CARIBBEAN MOON

CARIBBEAN MOON

MARJORIE CURTIS

THORNDIKE
CHIVERS

This Large Print edition is published by Thorndike Press, Waterville, Maine, USA and by BBC Audiobooks Ltd, Bath, England.

Thorndike Press is an imprint of The Gale Group.

Thorndike is a trademark and used herein under license.

ALL RIGHTS RESERVED

The text of this Large Print edition is unabridged.

Other aspects of the book may vary from the original edition.

Set in 16 pt. Plantin.

LIBRARY OF CONGRESS CATALOGING-IN-PUBLICATION DATA

Curtis, Marjorie.
  Caribbean moon / by Marjorie Curtis.
    p. cm.
  ISBN-13: 978-0-7862-9723-8 (lg. print : alk. paper)
  ISBN-10: 0-7862-9723-9 (lg. print : alk. paper)
  1. Large type books. 2. Caribbean Area — Fiction. I. Title.
PR6005.U762C37 2007
823'.912—dc22
                                        2007019074

BRITISH LIBRARY CATALOGUING-IN-PUBLICATION DATA AVAILABLE

Published in 2007 in the U.S. by arrangement with Robert Hale Limited.
Published in 2008 in the U.K. by arrangement with Robert Hale Limited.

U.K. Hardcover: 978 1 405 64146 3 (Chivers Large Print)
U.K. Softcover: 978 1 405 64147 0 (Camden Large Print)

Printed in the United States of America on permanent paper
10 9 8 7 6 5 4 3 2 1

CARIBBEAN MOON

CHAPTER ONE

Swooping to land on the runway at Melville Hall the small aeroplane nearly scraped the tips of the tall coconut palms as it came in from the sea. Emma stiffened with fear although she was excited at the novel experience. After the smoothness and speed of the jet plane which had brought her from London to Barbados this flight seemed much more adventurous.

From the air Dominica looked extremely mountainous with very few flat spaces and seemed about the size of the Isle of Man. The plane had descended like a flying insect into the bowl of mountains where the flattened air-strip was too small to accommodate larger aircraft.

Emma braced herself as the plane bounced a few times before checking its speed. Then when it had safely come to a halt she glanced at the man sitting beside her and smiled.

7

'I was afraid we wouldn't make it,' she said. 'It's a relief to be on the ground again.'

'It is rather frightening if you haven't experienced it before,' Gerald Forbes remarked. 'I thought the pilot brought us in very skilfully.'

'I expect he did. I'm becoming tired of travelling. It's good to know I've reached my destination.'

'Is anyone going to meet you?'

'I'm not sure,' she replied doubtfully. 'I sent a telegram when I reached Barbados and told them I would be on this flight. It depends whether they received it.'

'I'm going to Roseau. It's on the other side of the island. We are facing the Atlantic rollers here and you will find it very windy. The west coast is more protected.'

'I believe Belle Rive isn't far from Roseau,' Emma said.

'In that case if you don't want to go there at once why not put up in my hotel? It might be wiser for you to make a few enquiries about the place first.'

'It's kind of you but I don't want to hinder you. You have a job to do,' Emma replied.

'I don't intend to start until I've had a breather.'

He stared at her intently as if memorizing the small regular features, the silky chestnut hair and lovely brown eyes. Her skin was smooth and clear as a child's and he had to resist the impulse to stretch out a finger to caress her cheek.

Tearing his glance away, he said earnestly, 'If you decide not to come and you ever find yourself in some difficulty don't hesitate to contact me. You can reach me at the Fort Young Hotel near the harbour.'

On the landing-strip Emma looked about her with interest. The airport was almost enclosed by lofty palms curved inland by constant winds from the ocean. The air smelled of coconut oil and she could hear the crackle of dry leaves as the breeze stirred the trees. Above the control tower the flag was flapping vigorously against its pole. It was hot in the sun but not unpleasantly so and she was pleased that she had decided to wear her chocolate-brown slacks and cream silk blouse. It would have been a little too windy to wear a dress in comfort.

There were only four passengers besides Gerald and herself. He had travelled with her from London and they had become acquainted within a few minutes of leaving the airport. She had been grateful for his companionship for he had been to the Caribbean many times. He had told her a little about himself; that he was thirty-two, unmarried and employed by a lime juice manufacturer who had an estate and factories in Dominica.

He was the kind of man who would go unnoticed in a crowd. He was of medium height, rather thin with shoulders which stooped slightly. His face was angular, his hazel eyes serious beneath his high forehead and straight, fair hair.

After the brief formalities had been seen to they returned to the air-field where the taxi-bus was waiting. The other passengers had already seated themselves and the driver was climbing into his place.

'I shall have to go,' Gerald Forbes said reluctantly. 'I think you ought to come with me. You might get stranded here.'

'I'm not sure what to do,' she replied worriedly, glancing about her uncertainly.

Gerald was unwilling to urge her into the bus and watched her with concern. The driver was looking impatient and beckoning to them.

Gerald touched Emma's arm. 'Coming?' he asked.

'I might as well. I hate being so undecided.'

She was on the point of following him when a land-rover came at a fast speed along the perimeter of the surfaced apron.

It pulled up suddenly a few feet away from the taxi-bus. A tall, sun-tanned man in white climbed out and banged the door so violently that the vehicle shook. With a dark scowl on his lean face he strode swiftly across to the bus and spoke to the driver. Emma who had been watching him with wide, astonished eyes, saw the driver shrug his shoulders and point in her direction.

'It looks as if he's come for you,' Gerald remarked hurriedly. 'I will be off. Don't forget what I said.'

Emma nodded her head and murmured something. She had not expected to be met by a man so formidable and forceful and she scarcely noticed that Gerald had left her. Her heart quaked with an indefinable fear as she waited for the stranger to approach her.

'You are Miss Fielder?' he asked giving her a piercing stare from cool, blue eyes.

'Yes.' She wanted to ask him if he had been sent by the folk at Belle Rive but felt too nervous to question him. His scowl had vanished but she sensed an inner vexation. Obviously he had not wanted to meet her and could scarcely hide his annoyance.

'This your baggage?' he asked curtly. Picking up the two cases he carried them swiftly to the land-rover. There he glanced back

11

and frowned at her. 'Come along!' he said abruptly. 'What are you waiting for?'

After Gerald's good manners this man's lack of them was very noticeable. He did not bother to open the door for her. The handle was stiff and it took her all her strength to pull it open.

After carelessly dropping her cases in the back of the car he climbed into his seat and started the engine. Emma scrambled inside quickly as he appeared to be in such a hurry. In fact they left before the taxi-bus so she did not have a chance to wave to Gerald.

Her heart sank a little as she cast covert glances at the formidable profile of the man beside her. No one could have called him handsome. His nose was humped a little at the bridge as if it had been broken at some time. And there was a fine white scar running from the corner of his eye to his mouth. It was his jaw firm and decisive which made his face seem hard. It jutted a little too much for comfort. But when he turned his head to give her a brief glance she had to own that she had been criticizing him too harshly. His eyes were very blue beneath well-shaped, dark eyebrows and seemed to have a more friendly expression than when he had greeted her.

'What's the verdict?' he drawled in an amused, deep voice. 'Have you settled what kind of man I am?'

She laughed. 'Was it so obvious? I was wondering about your scar. It's hardly noticeable now but I expect it was pretty bad when it happened.'

'I got that when I went fishing with one of my buddies. He caught me instead of the fish. It was up north off the coast near Rollo Head. I had forgotten about it. It was nearly three years ago.'

'I'm sorry I seemed doubtful when we met. I hadn't expected to be met by . . .' She broke off in some confusion.

'A white man?' he said helping her out.

'Señora Guida led me to understand that the estate was run by Dominicans.'

'It is. I'm the manager.'

'I am honoured,' she said dryly.

He turned the wheel suddenly and violently missing a pot-hole by inches. He righted the vehicle and said gruffly:

'Weren't you told about me?'

Emma said cautiously, 'Señora Guida said that her niece had taken on a new manager.'

'I've been here nearly a year.'

The road was atrocious and several times Emma's head hit the roof. It was hilly and the road twisted continuously. Jungle clad mountains came in for a brief glimpse every now and then but for most of the way it was dense bush and rain forest.

After successfully avoiding yet another pot-hole the man ejaculated, 'One of these darn holes was the reason I was so late. I got a rear wheel stuck and it took me half an hour to lever it out.'

'Are all the roads like this?'

'I guess so. This is better than some.'

Emma asked quietly, 'What is your name?'

'Steve Randell.'

'Are you an American?'

'Canadian. You sound English.'

She laughed softly. 'I ought to. I've lived in London all my life.'

'That can't be very long.' His eyes glinted as he turned to glance at her. 'The Guida's taste is improving. The others were not so easy on the eye.'

'What others?' she asked in a puzzled voice.

'Never mind. Look over there on your left. That's the Carib Reservation.'

'Are they the Indians? I didn't think there were any left.'

'This is about the only place in the Caribbean. They fought hard to keep their land. I'm afraid most of them were shipped to British Honduras.'

'Is it true that they were Cannibals?'

'Columbus thought so. They were fierce fighters. He discovered the island on a Sunday hence the Latin name Dominica. That was in 1493. A long time ago.' He chuckled. 'The Caribs had one custom which some men might find highly useful now. They would kill their wives if they were unfaithful.'

'Women with erring husbands might find it advantageous more often,' Emma said dryly.

Steve grinned. 'Nowadays the Carib men and women lead quiet lives,' he said. 'They live in shacks with small flower gardens, grow bananas, make baskets and canoes and go fishing. However they still enjoy getting drunk on rum.'

'Do the children go to school?'

'Sure. They have one in the Reservation. They can catch a bus at Pagua Bay and shop in Roseau. I have found that they are real nice people and their kids are grand.'

Emma was beginning to change her opinion of him. He could not be too bad if he liked the Caribs and had a soft spot for the children. And he was an interesting companion. He had enlivened the journey with his slant on Dominica.

'Who was the guy you were talking to?'

Steve asked abruptly.

'Gerald Forbes. I met him on the plane from London.'

'I thought he looked familiar. Isn't he connected with a lime manufacturer?'

'Yes. He has been here before. He's staying in Roseau. Is Belle Rive near there?'

'Not far as the crow flies but this is a mountainous island. It's all rain forest and rivers and everything is on the slope.'

'It makes the scenery very beautiful.'

'Be careful! Dominica makes a habit of enticing people to stay.'

She asked with amused curiosity, 'Is that what happened to you?'

'Maybe. Don't expect a gay life at Belle Rive. The property is a mass of banana, coconut, lime and tropical trees. Throw in a few streams and small rivers and you have the picture.'

Steve was driving faster now and Emma thought it safer not to distract his attention by talking. She let her mind drift back to the last few weeks when she had been contemplating this trip.

Emma was a receptionist at an hotel in Knightsbridge and during the two years she had been there, she had met many interesting people. The Guidas had arrived nine months ago after spending six months on the Riviera. At first Emma had taken little notice of them for they went out a good deal. Then one day the manager asked her to do some typing for Señor Guida and she spent a few hours each day for a week working in his suite.

She took a liking to Señora Guida who obviously wanted to be friendly. Emma who lived in the hotel did feel lonely sometimes and she was grateful when the Guidas asked her out to dinner or took her to a theatre with them. The Señora often spoke of her home in Dominica and discussed the problems of running an estate.

'Wouldn't it be easier if you lived there?' Emma asked one day when she was having tea with them in their suite.

'Yes, it would,' Señora Guida replied. 'We intend to go back one day when my husband is well enough. He is the reason we left. He had been ill for so long that his doctor suggested we lived abroad for a while to see if a change of climate might help.'

'I'm sorry. I do hope Señor Guida soon recovers,' Emma said feeling rather awkward because he was in the room.

'He has improved. Everything would be fine if we didn't have to worry about my niece and the estate. Aimee is usually sensible but my husband and I were deeply shocked when we learned that she had got rid of the manager we engaged. It was so foolish of her. Now she is alone at Belle Rive with some strange man she has employed. Armand, the manager we left there, was married and his wife acted as a companion for Aimee. It is not fitting that a young girl should live alone especially when we do not know what type of person this other man is.'

'I'm surprised your niece could do that without your permission.'

Señora Guida smiled grimly. 'She forced my hand. With no other man to take Armand's place I had to accept the man she had employed. He has written to me and I have confirmed his appointment but I am not happy about it.'

Señor Guida, a thin, sallow-skinned man with melancholy eyes, said sadly, 'It is very upsetting, my dear, but what can we do?'

His wife looked at Emma thoughtfully. 'Perhaps the answer lies with Emma. She and Aimee would get on well together, I'm sure.' She smiled as she went on, 'How would you like to have a few months in Dominica?' She raised her hand to silence Emma who was about to speak. 'Don't give me your answer now. Think on it. I don't want you to decide hastily.'

18

'It's very tempting,' Emma said slowly. 'I would have to give up my job.'

'I could ask the manager to keep it open for you,' the Señora said. 'He could get a temporary girl for two months.'

Emma shook her head. 'Actually I have been thinking of leaving. I thought I would work in an office for a while. The hours would be easier.'

'You wouldn't have much to do in Dominica. I will pay your fare and give you the same salary as you are getting now.'

'How old is your niece?' Emma asked.

'Twenty. You are twenty-four I believe. You will be a good influence on Aimee. Don't be afraid that she won't welcome you. She's a friendly girl.'

'I was wondering whether she would be annoyed at having me there.'

'I do hope you will decide to go. It will set my mind at rest. You will be able to tell me what kind of man she has employed and if the estate is being cared for.'

Emma glanced at her doubtfully. 'It might look all right to me. I haven't any experience about farms or estates.'

'Don't worry about it. If you do notice anything peculiar or something you think is not correct you can let me know and I will deal with it.'

'It sounds rather like spying,' Emma said dubiously.

'You needn't report to me if you feel it's distasteful,' Señora Guida said kindly. 'Please give it your consideration. I do want you to go. Aimee needs someone there and you are an intelligent young woman.'

It did not take Emma long to make up her mind. She went home for the week-end and discussed it with her parents who thought it a marvellous opportunity for her. When she returned to the hotel she told the Guidas that she was willing to go to Dominica for two months and gave in her notice to the manager.

'How long do the Guidas expect you to stay?'

Steve's question brought her out of her reverie with a start and she saw that they were crossing a narrow bridge over a swiftly running stream which cut through the rain forest.

'I have arranged to stay two months,' Emma told him.

'That takes you to the beginning of June if you last,' he drawled.

She gave him a quick glance of surprise. 'Is there any reason why I shouldn't stay?'

'I can think of a few. The Guidas take a lot for granted.'

'I didn't think you knew them.'

'I don't and from what I've been told about them I'm not sure I want to meet them,' Steve said scathingly.

'How can you sum people up before you've even seen them?'

'Real easy. Actions speak louder than words. I've seen what they did to Aimee. It's unbelievable the ruthlessness of some folk.'

Emma replied in a shocked voice, 'I don't believe it! They are kind people.'

'Is that a fact,' he said faintly mocking. 'We shall have to differ over that. I stick to what I say. You can believe what you like.'

'Thanks,' she retorted dryly.

He cast a swift glance at her and smiled. 'You are finding all this real strange, I guess. What did you do in London?'

'I was a receptionist in an hotel. That's how I met the Guidas.'

'A luxury hotel?'

She chuckled. 'I wouldn't call it that. It was quite ordinary. The food was excellent and the hotel comfortable. We had many foreign visitors. The Guidas stayed quite a few months.'

'You do surprise me! I imagined they were living it up.'

'It's expensive for anyone living in

London.' Emma was not going to allow him to criticize her friends without some defence.

'They could have stayed here and spent about a quarter of what they do,' he said curtly.

'That ought not to concern us,' she said firmly. Then determined to change the subject she exclaimed, 'What magnificent trees! I noticed a lot of them were tall but these are exceptional.'

'You will see plenty if you stay long enough,' he drawled carelessly. 'These are *chataignier* — chestnut you would call them — then there's teak, ebony, locust and of course, palm. In other areas there's the cannonball and cashew nut amongst a few others.'

'You obviously know about trees. Some of the trunks are hidden beneath the ivy. It's tremendously thick, isn't it?'

'The Caribs use it for making baskets. It's one of the plagues on the island. When that's around we know the soil is useless especially when there are those huge ferns in the vicinity.'

'There's more to it than meets the eye then,' Emma remarked. 'What a pity when it's so beautiful.'

'The same could apply to the human

race,' Steve drawled cynically.

She chuckled. 'Evidently you've been unlucky with your relationships. I've always found people fairly favourable.'

'Bully for you!' he said mockingly. 'I've seen more of the world than you have. When you've been here a little longer you may change your views.'

'I hope not.' She frowned. 'Are you trying to warn me about something or someone?'

'Maybe. You seem a little naïve.'

'I'm not! You do tend to sum people up unfairly. Just because I give them the benefit of the doubt you assume I'm simple.'

Steve grinned and shrugged his broad shoulders. 'Okay, I give in. I was warning you for your own good. I prefer not to have folk trample over me.'

She laughed. 'That might be difficult to do.'

He smiled as he accelerated at the approach of a steep hill and drawled, 'I guess so. I've survived so far.'

'There's hardly any breeze here yet, we have climbed so many hills,' Emma remarked.

'That's because we have entered the Roseau valley and are on the leeward side of the island which is protected from the Atlantic winds. We haven't much farther to go now.'

'We seem to have been travelling a long time yet from the air Dominica looked so tiny.'

'It is. It's only twenty-nine miles long and about sixteen miles in breadth. It's the winding twisting roads which give you the impression we are travelling miles.' He turned his head and smiled at her. 'I didn't reckon on having such an interesting companion. The other young woman I had to meet three months ago was full of grumbles. She complained all the way across the island.'

'Why did she come?' Emma asked curiously.

'I never asked her,' he replied carelessly. 'I guess it was lucky for us that she didn't stay long. She had a row with Esmeralda, packed her bag and left.'

'Who is Esmeralda?'

Steve laughed. 'She is Belle Rive. Don't ask me to describe her. I couldn't do her justice. She's been there ever since the original building was erected. She thinks she runs the place. I've had a few battles with her.'

'Who was the victor?'

'Neither of us. Nowadays we eye each other warily.'

'Is she old?'

'Sure. Aimee's father had the wooden house pulled down after a hurricane destroyed most of it. It's made of stone blocks now; not so picturesque but a darn sight safer.'

'I thought it might be one of those grand old mansions with wooden balconies and gabled roofs.'

'It used to be. I guess you are in for a disappointment. It looks quite modern.'

'What a pity! I was looking forward to taking photographs of it,' Emma said.

Steve grinned. 'Get Esmeralda's permission first otherwise she will suspect you are practising white man's voodoo.'

Emma looked startled. 'Does that go on still?'

'It crops up occasionally. Don't sound so alarmed. To a non-believer it has no effect.'

'I've heard differently. Terrible things can happen if someone hates you.'

'Then it's not likely to happen to you,' Steve drawled in a deep amused voice. 'Who could take a dislike to a harmless little creature who thinks only good of her fellow men. Aimee's going to love you, that's for sure!'

Emma eyed his bronzed profile with slight resentment. The trouble is I'm never sure when he's joking or serious, she thought. He might even be enjoying the knowledge that Aimee and Esmeralda are going to be annoyed because I've come. Their other visitor didn't stay long. Is it going to be the same for me?

The land was looking more cultivated now and she guessed that they were nearing their destination. She recognized some of the crops; maize, sugar cane and various root vegetables.

'Why has this strip been left for the weeds?' she asked thinking that they had been silent long enough.

'That's indigo not weed. We grow a little of everything. I've tried to make the estate self-sufficient. That's why you can see so many different vegetables. We sell some also along with the grapefruit, orange, lime and coconut. It sounds a lot for a small estate but we get good crops in each small area. It's packed in tightly as you can see. But it does create problems for it's not easy to handle.'

Emma scarcely noticed the house as Steve drove the car slowly over the grassy, unmade road. Her gaze was entirely taken up with the mountain which sheltered the house and valley. But when she climbed out and the background was no longer so noticeable, she felt quite impressed by the L-shaped, white stone building with its louvred shutters at the unglazed windows. They were rounded at the top and looked rather like church apertures. The arched door and sloping roof increased this effect. Clumps of hibiscus grew near the house and vines of jessamine and bougainvillaea covered parts of the walls. A few of them had started to flower but Emma guessed that it would be days perhaps weeks before they were in full bloom.

The interior was cool and airy. Steve who had led the way inside put down Emma's cases and frowned.

'Where the devil are they?' he muttered then called out in a loud voice, 'Aimee!'

A door opened at the far end of the living-room and a young woman moved gracefully towards them. She was slim and pretty, dressed in a flowered cotton dress which showed off her bare, coffee-coloured arms and legs. Her black hair was shiny and smooth, tied back with a satin ribbon which looked new and matched the red in her dress. Emma was reminded of Señora Guida as she came closer. The girl had a flattish nose and oval-shaped face similar to her aunt. Her skin was clearer and more youthful but there was a striking resemblance especially about the eyes which were large, very dark and widely-spaced.

'I thought you would have heard us arrive, Aimee,' Steve drawled. 'Aren't you going to welcome Miss Fielder?'

The girl's lack of warmth was so noticeable that Emma shook hands with her awkwardly. Señora Guida had been so certain that Aimee would be pleased to see her but the girl showed no sign that Emma was welcome.

Steve frowned and said curtly, 'Miss Fielder is tired after her journey, Aimee. I'm sure she would like a drink.'

Aimee nodded. 'Will you stay, Steve? The coffee is hot.'

'I guess you can manage without me. I've lost too much time already.'

Emma said pleasantly, 'Thanks for meeting me, Mr Randell. I'm sorry I took you away from your work.'

His thick, dark eyebrows rose a fraction as he smiled. 'It was no trouble. I enjoyed it. You will soon settle down. Give Aimee a little time to get used to you. She's used to being on her own.' He gave the girl a straight, meaningful look. 'Do your best, Aimee. Make her feel at home.'

The girl seemed surprised. 'Yes, Steve, if you say so,' she muttered.

28

'I will be off then. See you tonight, Miss Fielder.'

Emma felt rather lost after he had gone. The room seemed cold and cheerless. She had not liked Steve Randell overmuch but now without him she was conscious of feeling lonely and a little afraid.

CHAPTER TWO

'I never drank coffee much until Steve came,' Aimee remarked as she set down a tray with a small jug of scalded milk, a cup half filled with black coffee and a bowl of sugar on it. 'Would you serve yourself?'

'Thank you.' Emma seated herself on the low settee and added milk and sugar to the coffee. 'Mr Randell said he was a Canadian. I expect that's why he likes coffee.'

'That is true,' Aimee said expressionlessly. She was standing close to the settee staring down at Emma with a solemn expression on her oval face. Her hands were clasped tightly behind her back as if she had been trained to wait thus for a dismissal.

The coffee tasted delicious and after a few sips Emma's confidence returned. She was a little amused at the behaviour of the young girl and wished that she would not eye her so guardedly.

'Why don't you have some with me?' she

asked giving Aimee a warm friendly smile. 'I don't think I've ever had coffee in the afternoon but I'm enjoying it. It really is very good.'

Aimee's grave face brightened and she sat down in a chair near Emma. 'Steve taught me to make it the way he likes it. I had some after my lunch.' She hesitated then asked politely, 'Would you like something to eat?'

'No thank you. I had lunch early before I left. Do tell me about yourself. There's so much I want to know.'

The guarded expression returned to Aimee's dark eyes. 'Why?' she asked bluntly. 'What exactly do you want? Why doesn't my aunt ask her own questions? Why did she have to send you?'

Emma put her cup down carefully astounded by this unexpected attack. 'I've upset you. I am sorry. Your aunt didn't send me to interrogate you. It was clumsy of me.' Emma smiled. 'I've never been abroad before so naturally I'm very interested in everything. Perhaps if I tell you something about myself you will understand. Your aunt and uncle were staying at the hotel where I worked as a receptionist. We became friendly and she often talked about you. She was very worried because you were on your own. Then one day she asked me if I would come here as your companion for two months.'

'You knew my uncle well?'

There was such a strange expression in the girl's large, dark eyes that Emma hesitated before replying. It looked as if Aimee was set on being unfriendly. I don't have to stay, she thought feeling a twinge of dismay. If the girl doesn't want me here it would be wiser to leave right now.

She said carefully, 'I was more friendly with your aunt. I found Señor Guida rather shy and difficult to get to know. I felt sorry for Señora Guida. I sensed she was lonely and homesick. One of the reasons I agreed to come here was so that she would not be so worried about you. She loves you very much.'

Aimee nodded. 'Sometimes I like her also.' She paused then continued wistfully, 'I want to believe you. You are nicer than the others.'

'You have had other companions?'

Aimee's lips parted showing her even white teeth. It was the first smile she had given Emma who had been trying so hard to make the girl relax.

'You are the third,' Aimee said. 'I told Aunt Sophie not to send anyone.'

Emma eyed her curiously. 'Why didn't they stay?'

'They were different to you.' She broke

off then said hurriedly, 'It is embarrassing. My aunt sent them here to get rid of them. It was her way of protecting her marriage.'

Emma stared at her in shocked amazement. 'You think they were Señor Guida's girl friends?'

'I'm certain of it. My aunt bribed them. She is very clever. Dominica is a long way from London. That is why they did not stay long. They had a vacation then left. Ask Steve if you don't believe me. He will tell you I'm right.'

Emma said doubtfully, 'Señor Guida seemed such a pleasant, quiet man.'

'Yes, he can be charming. It's obvious you did not know him. He has a selfish, cruel streak. I ought to know I have suffered enough from his callousness.'

'I could have been misled,' Emma said thoughtfully. 'As I said I didn't have very much to do with him. If it's true what you say then I can understand why you were reluctant to have me here.' She smiled. 'If it had been me I would have shown my antagonism.'

'It would have served no purpose,' Aimee said seriously. 'It is lonely here. Belle Rive soon drives away unsuitable people.'

'I see,' Emma replied slowly. 'When you heard I was coming you expected that to happen to me.'

'I thought you would be like the other girls.' Aimee smiled. 'I hope you will stay longer. You have been more frank with me. Aunt Sophie can be very irritating. I told her I didn't want a companion but she takes no notice. I do hope you won't take offence. It's nothing personal. Now I've met you I'm beginning to change my mind. I do get lonely sometimes. The other girls didn't want to be friendly and they tried to order me around. They didn't understand our ways so naturally we clashed sometimes.'

'I expect you did. I haven't come here to keep you in order.' Emma laughed. 'I'm not the bossy type and it would take more nerve than I have. Also I'm not much older than you are. If you discover I'm getting too big for my shoes then you will have to tell me so. I'm curious by nature so if you think I'm too inquisitive and ask too many questions a hint from you will stop me.'

'I'm so glad we've had this talk.' Aimee stood up and moved away from the settee. 'I will show you your room. It is very small but it has its own bathroom.'

Emma followed her through a bead curtain to the other end of the house turning at right angles to walk down a long corridor.

'It's very cool,' she remarked. 'I thought it

34

would be much warmer than it is.'

'The mountain protects us from the sun. The original house was wooden with three storeys. It was a terrible place to keep clean. I wasn't very upset when the hurricane flattened it.'

'Has this one been built long?'

'Five years. My mother was French and she insisted on having a modern house.' Aimee opened a louvred door and waited for Emma to pass inside. 'As you can see there are no curtains in here. The stained wood floor is easily cleaned.'

Emma thought the room looked very austere but she made no comment. A flowered cotton quilt covered the single bed which had a reed mat at the side. There was a rail for clothes, a small chest of drawers with a mirror above and a tiny table between the window and the bed.

'It's very nice,' she said smilingly.

'Your bathroom is across the corridor.' Aimee smiled and spoke proudly. 'We have three altogether.'

'That's astonishing,' Emma told her. 'I always thought that Dominica was a backward country.'

'There are plenty of people who haven't one at all,' Aimee said seriously. 'My father made money and my mother spent it; wisely

I think because now the house belongs to me.'

Emma looked puzzled. 'I thought the estate belonged to the Guidas.'

'They can't prove that. My father took over the estate when his father died. Aunt Sophie ought to have complained then. She and my father were the only children. In French law if there is no will the children are joint owners. That is why the Guidas say the estate belongs to them now.'

'That seems unfair to you. Did they take control after your father died?'

'Yes but I don't intend that they shall have it. I can't do much until I'm free of Aunt Sophie. She's my guardian until I'm twenty-one. That's why I said my mother was wise when she insisted that I be left the house. I have the deeds for it so the Guidas can't turn me out.'

'Why didn't your aunt make a claim before?'

'Her husband didn't want to run the estate. He's bone lazy and he couldn't bear the thought of being cooped up here. If they had cut the land in two he would have had to have another house built. At that time they didn't have enough money. My father gave them money to keep them quiet and it worked fairly well until recently.'

Emma frowned. 'It sounds very complicated. Do all the profits go to them now?'

'Since my father died. Steve has to give me enough to run the house.'

'Didn't you have anyone you could go to for advice?'

Aimee nodded. 'My father's solicitor was very kind. He said I ought to wait until I'm twenty-one.'

'When did your mother die?'

'Three years ago. She had a long illness. The following year my father was drowned in a fishing accident.'

'That's very sad,' Emma said giving her a compassionate glance. 'What a terrible shock for you!'

'Yes. I miss them both very much.' Aimee straightened her thin shoulders. 'I have been talking too much. It is unusual for me to unburden myself to a stranger. You are too sympathetic. I have asked you nothing about yourself.'

Emma smiled. 'My life seems very insignificant. I haven't done much. I lived with my parents until I left school. Then I took up hotel work and lived away from home.'

'Being a receptionist must have been interesting.'

'It was sometimes. I had to work hard and the hours were long. I never knew when I might have to give up my free time.'

'You can do as you like here but there's not much to do. Roseau is our nearest town.'

'Do you help on the estate?' Emma asked.

'Sometimes but usually there is enough to keep me busy in the house. I have the meals to get. Steve has breakfast and dinner here.'

'Does he sleep in the house?'

'Yes. He has a room nearer the main part farther up the corridor.'

'Do you have help in the house?'

'Occasionally. If Steve invites his friends, Esmeralda employs a girl to give us a hand.'

'Mr Randell mentioned her. He said she has been here a long time.'

'She was with my parents when I was born. She is a Carib woman and worked for my grandfather. She is old now and does not do much. She can be a little frightening but she means well.'

'I expect you were grateful for her company when you were left alone.'

'Yes. She has been a great comfort.' Aimee turned towards the door. 'I noticed Steve has brought in your baggage. I will leave you to unpack. Please make yourself at home. You can consider the bathroom yours. Steve uses the one near him and I have my own.'

Emma smiled to herself when she was

alone. Aimee was so proud of her three bathrooms. I don't blame her, she thought, after seeing all those shacks on the drive across the island I can well understand her pride. Steve mentioned that the majority of the shack dwellers used rivers and streams for bathing, washing and drinking! I hope Aimee boils the water she uses for cooking. She seems a very sensible girl so I expect she does. I felt so sorry for her, losing both parents like that and having a relative step in and take over the estate. I suppose Señora Guida really thinks she's entitled to it. She seemed such a generous-minded woman. Now I've listened to Aimee's account I feel rather bewildered. The girl speaks English very well and I got the impression that she'd been well-educated. Her mother was responsible for that I imagine.

After she had taken a bath and put on fresh clothes Emma was not sure what to do. It seemed so quiet after the London hotel. I won't bother Aimee again, she thought. I expect she's preparing the dinner and I might get in the way. Tomorrow I will offer to help. I ought to let Señora Guida know that I've arrived safely. I have some air-mail letters. Someone told me all the mail goes by air so if I haven't enough I can use my other notepaper.

The time went quickly. She wrote very little to the Señora because as yet the information she had gleaned was unsubstantiated. Steve Randell seemed pleasant enough but first impressions could be wrong. Also after what Aimee had told her she felt rather puzzled wondering whether Señora Guida was entitled to know how Aimee and Steve were managing. She is my employer and she's Aimee's guardian so I ought to be loyal to her, Emma told herself doubtfully. All she really wanted to know was whether Aimee was safe and well and whether the new manager could be trusted. After I have been here for a while I shall be able to reassure her. I'm sure everything is all right.

After that she wrote a lengthy letter to her parents and another to a girl friend. She was sealing the envelopes when she heard a jeep drive up and feeling curious glanced out of the window. Steve was climbing out of the jeep. He was wearing shorts and a brown shirt and looked tired. He did not glance in her direction as he strolled towards the house. He had some papers under his arm and carelessly swung a dead brown rabbit which dangled from his hand.

Emma waited until she heard him bang the door to his room before she emerged. It was ten minutes or so after his entry into the house and she guessed he had gone to the kitchen first.

When she did finally go through the bead curtain she wished that she had waited a little longer for the first person she saw was Esmeralda. It could only be her, Emma thought as she watched the old woman move slowly round the table setting out knives and forks.

She was a big woman, flat-chested with scrawny arms and hands. Her dark brown face was full with deep grooves running from the flat nose to the fleshy chin. She was dressed in a long, white gown. It had a small collar above the V-neck which showed her prominent breast bone. Her hair was hidden by a tightly bound, white scarf tied in a knot on top of her head. It looked strange set like that above her ears and tight over her eyebrows.

It's stupid to be frightened of her, Emma told herself encouragingly for she had felt herself tremble at the sight of the old woman. She began to move forward trying to appear as natural as possible.

'Good evening,' she said politely. 'Can I help you do that?'

Esmeralda turned abruptly to stare at her. A cold clammy sensation slowly seeped into

Emma's slender body. She wanted to turn away but was unable to move. One look at those wrinkled, heavy-lidded eyes and she was held rooted to the spot. The woman was so relaxed that no one could have believed or realized the hypnotic power she was directing at Emma. Then the slanting, black eyes glinted and became menacing. The spell was broken and Emma, dazed and frightened, moved away.

Aimee came from the kitchen carrying a huge tureen of steaming soup. She set it in the centre of the table then turned to Emma.

'This is Esmeralda. Has she spoken to you yet?'

Emma shook her head. Her mouth felt dry and her tongue seemed swollen. It was impossible to speak.

'Don't be shy. Esmeralda is a friendly person,' Aimee said. 'She speaks very good English.' When Emma did not reply she went on, 'I shall only be a few minutes. Seat yourself at the table.'

As Emma was not sure where to sit and had no desire to ask the old woman she wandered over to the settee at the other end of the room and sat down. Then Steve came in and she breathed more freely. He looked fresh and clean in white slacks and shirt and she could smell the pleasant fragrance of his after-shave lotion.

His eyes twinkled when he noticed the old woman. 'I reckon I'm in time tonight, Esmeralda,' he drawled. 'You can't complain about my manners now.'

She nodded gravely. 'It's your favourite *crapaud* tonight, Mr Steve.'

'Is that a fact!' He flashed a swift smile at Emma and added succinctly, 'Mountain chicken.'

Emma heard the woman give a throaty chuckle and she moved uneasily. The incident a few minutes ago had taken all her confidence away.

The soup was delicious but Emma thought it prudent not to ask what it was made of. It had a flavour she had not tasted before. The *crapaud* whatever it was, did taste like chicken. She noticed that Aimee and Steve were casting frequent glances at her to see if she was eating it and guessed that it was not chicken at all.

'That was marvellous!' she exclaimed sincerely when she had finished. 'You are a good cook, Aimee.'

The girl nodded and looked pleased. 'I ought to be. I've had enough lessons. My mother insisted that I learned the art. She taught me everything she knew. It's time and patience mostly.'

For dessert they had a lemon soufflé which really did melt in the mouth. Asked if she wished for any more, Emma shook her head.

'I've eaten far more than I normally do,' she explained.

Steve glanced at Aimee and raised his glass of wine. 'To a first rate cook! You've excelled yourself. No wonder we are putty in your hands and slaves for you to command!'

Aimee giggled and clapped her hands. 'You are funny! I'm not that good. But I'm pleased that Emma enjoyed it. It's a refreshing change to see a newcomer eat without querying what the food is composed of.'

With Esmeralda sitting a few feet away I wouldn't have had the nerve, Emma thought. If I hadn't been so hungry she might have put me off. The other two don't appear to mind her. Perhaps I'm too sensitive. If I'm to stay here I shall have to get used to her.

Steve was saying in an amused voice, 'You were unlucky with the other young women.' He grinned and turned to Emma. 'After their first meal they insisted on eating plainer foods. The last one lived on scrambled eggs and toast.'

Emma smiled. 'I used to be apprehensive. Since I left home I've had some very strange meals. We have so many foreign restaurants in London now.'

'You were taken out a lot?' Steve asked as he handed her a cup of coffee.

'Frequently. Working in an hotel brought me into contact with people.'

'You've had *crapaud* before then?'

'I may have. It wasn't chicken, was it?'

Aimee chuckled. 'It was frog. Are you shocked?'

'That's why I thought I had tasted it before! But your *crapaud* is more succulent.'

'We don't rear much cattle on the island,' Aimee explained. 'We have to rely on wild meat. We have rabbits, pigs, partridge, duck and turtle to name a few. We keep our own chickens and grow our vegetables.'

Emma smiled. 'It was turtle soup we had tonight?'

'Yes. Now that is surprising! Not many people guess right first time.'

'You've scored with Aimee,' Steve drawled. 'She will enjoy cooking for you.'

'I hope she will allow me to help her. I won't have much to do otherwise.'

She heard Esmeralda grunt and mutter something and cast a swift apprehensive glance in her direction. Steve laughed and wagged a finger at the old woman.

'That was real naughty of you, Esmeralda. Emma is Aimee's guest. We want her to stay so don't try to frighten her.'

Esmeralda stared at him expressionlessly then in a dignified manner turned her back on him. A few seconds later she moved stiffly and slowly out of the room to the kitchen.

Aimee exclaimed in distress, 'You've upset her, Steve!'

'I don't care if I have,' he said curtly. 'It's time someone rebuked her. She can't be allowed to mutter threats at random.'

'She doesn't mean any harm.' Aimee frowned. 'I will speak to her and try to explain. She's always suspicious of newcomers. It's only because she's loyal to me.'

'She's a domineering old woman,' Steve said. 'I wouldn't say anything to her, Aimee. Let her stew in her own juice.'

The girl laughed. 'What an expression! If Emma will forgive and make allowances for Esmeralda's behaviour, I won't talk to her. She will only become angry and think I'm criticizing her. I don't want her going to her witch doctor again.'

'Does she believe in sorcerers?' Emma asked curiously.

'She certainly does. I've tried to show her

how silly her black magic is but she's very obstinate. She won't allow a qualified doctor to examine her. When she's ill she treats herself with potions and symbols.'

Steve laughed. 'It's all a load of nonsense. She uses her black magic to gain power over her weaker opponents.'

'There's more to it than that,' Aimee said seriously as she began to put the cups on the tray. 'I wouldn't dismiss it so lightly.'

A little reluctantly Emma followed the girl into the kitchen. Although she had not mentioned it to the others she was rather scared of the old woman. But much to her relief Esmeralda was no longer in the kitchen and Emma breathed more easily.

'Shall I wash?' she asked as she went to the stainless steel sink unit.

'If you want to,' Aimee replied cheerfully. 'There's plenty of hot water. I will dry the things and put them away.'

'Doesn't Esmeralda help you?'

'Not in here. She gets in my way. As a matter of fact she prefers to look after the house. You needn't worry about her. She's gone for a walk. She likes being out at night. You won't see her again this evening.'

'It gets dark very quickly, doesn't it?' Emma remarked as she washed the glasses and rinsed them. 'The sun was setting when

Mr Randell came in. A few minutes later I had to switch on the light.'

'We don't have a twilight. Night comes without warning. My mother used to miss the transitional period.'

'I shall have to remember that if I'm out. I might get scared if I was in the rain forest.'

'It can be frightening. It's difficult for strangers to believe that they can get lost when they are only a few miles away from home. Some parts of the interior have never been explored. It's so mountainous and forested. Even around here the trees are dense and the bush inpenetrable. It's safer to keep to a track or path. If you are lost someone will find you then.'

'It's half past ten already!' Emma exclaimed when they had finished. 'The time has gone quickly.'

'What would you like to do? We can sit and talk, play cards or listen to the radio.'

'I feel rather tired. I would prefer to go to bed.'

'I don't mind. Steve has gone to his room. He prefers to work there. He has papers and contracts to look at.'

'I will see you in the morning then,' Emma said.

Light shone from Steve's door as she passed but she could hear no noise. Gain-ing her room she swiftly undressed, put on her flimsy dressing-gown and went across to the bathroom.

When she returned she carefully turned down the quilt then threw back the bedclothes. Something black and shiny stirred and before she could take hold of herself she had uttered a loud shriek of dismay. Scuttling away from the light were two enormous beetles, six inches long at least!

She cowered against the wall, white faced and sick with fright. The door opened and Steve rushed in.

After a swift glance at her ashen face he said urgently, 'What's the matter? Are you ill?'

She pointed to the bed and in a shaky voice murmured, 'There's two horrible insects there.'

He turned sharply and examined the empty bed. 'There's nothing there now.' He lifted the pillow gingerly and let it fall quickly. 'I see what you mean,' he said coolly.

Swinging round he grabbed the towel she had hung over the back of the chair then twisted away from her to scoop up the offending insects. Then with the towel screwed up into a ball he went out.

Emma gasped with relief. She was feeling

so shaken that she was unable to move. She stared at the bed wondering how she was ever going to summon up enough nerve to sleep there.

When Steve came back his face was tight with anger. 'Soon got rid of them,' he said grimly. 'They were saw-beetles. I don't know how the dickens they got in the house. I've never seen them around here before. We get plenty of smaller luminous ones but those particular kind don't come from around here.' He gave her a glance of compassion. 'Nasty experience for you on your first night.'

She said shakily, 'I feel like making it my last.'

'That's the object of the game I reckon,' he said with a dark frown.

'Thanks for coming so quickly.'

He grinned. 'Your shriek would have awakened the dead. I'm surprised Aimee didn't hear you.'

'I expect she's in the kitchen.' She was becoming conscious of her undressed state and pulled her gown closer.

He was eyeing her doubtfully. 'You don't look too grand. What's bothering you?' He saw her expression as she looked at the bed and his face lightened. 'I get it. You don't want to sleep there.'

She smiled ruefully. 'It's silly, I know but I'm sure I shall imagine something is still there.'

'That's easily remedied. You can help me strip the bed.'

He made a thorough job of it even to turning the mattress. Then he rolled the sheets and pillowcases up and went out with them.

When he returned with clean ones Emma ejaculated, 'You needn't have done that. Aimee will think I'm an awful nuisance.'

'Aimee can think what she likes. We can't have you having a sleepless night.'

His protectiveness did much to restore her confidence. She had not expected him to be so kind and understanding.

'It is very good of you,' she said gratefully giving him a sweet smile and a softened glance from her lovely eyes.

'Think nothing of it,' he said carelessly. 'I guess I understood how you felt. I have two sisters back home. It's not the first time I've had to rescue damsels from obnoxious insects.'

'I bet they weren't as large as they were.'

His grin faded and his face became grave. 'No. You behaved well considering. I think most girls would have become hysterical or fainted.'

She smiled faintly. 'I nearly did. It was the shock.'

'You needn't worry now. You can sleep with an easy mind.'

He was about to open the door when she said anxiously, 'Do you have to tell Aimee? Will she notice the sheets have been changed?'

'I doubt it.' He frowned. 'I won't mention it if that's what you want.'

'It might upset her.' Emma hesitated then said, 'I think someone put those creatures there to frighten me.'

'The same thought had crossed my mind.' He smiled grimly. 'We can't let it ride. I may find it necessary to explain to Aimee.'

'You do whatever you think is best. Did the same thing happen to the other girls?'

'Not to my knowledge. If it had I'm sure I would have been told.' He frowned. 'Evidently someone has decided you are going to be difficult to frighten off.'

'Esmeralda?'

'It looks like it. Watch your step little one. She's a nasty enemy.'

Emma sighed. 'I just don't understand. Why does she want to get rid of me? Why did she frighten off the other girls?'

'We don't know that she did. I can only guess. They were suspicious all the time they were here, tasted the food gingerly before they ate it and spoke to Aimee as if she was beneath their contempt. I couldn't make it out. Aimee was convinced that they were her uncle's girl friends.'

'You didn't go along with that?'

Steve smiled. 'I thought his taste was poor.'

She stared at him accusingly. 'You thought I might be the same. That's why you said the Señor's taste was improving.'

'Correction! I said the Guidas' taste was improving. I don't go along with Aimee's theory. Anyway that wouldn't cause Esmeralda to become awkward. She's very fond of Aimee and looks upon Belle Rive as her home. She dislikes the Guidas and is suspicious because you were sent by them.'

'The Señora is worried about her niece.'

'Sure. I can understand that. Don't worry your pretty little head. Things will be mighty different from now on.'

Emma felt far from confident after he had gone. Evidently he suspected further unpleasant things to happen. I can't see myself lasting any longer than the other girls, she thought unhappily. I think the Señora ought to have told me that she had sent other young women here and warned me. But then I suppose I wouldn't have come and

Señora Guida knew that.

Yawning with weariness she moved over to the bed and gingerly climbed in leaving her dressing-gown on. She felt in need of the extra protection even though she knew the room was free of insects.

It took her a long time to fall asleep after she had switched off the light. And even then her mind was tormented by malicious images with cavernous eyes and mouths. After feverishly tossing and turning for most of the night she awoke to find the sun was up. The cocks were crowing and birds twittering in the cassia tree close to her window.

CHAPTER THREE

A young girl Emma had not seen before came in with a cup of tea on a tray. She was brown-skinned, pleasing to look at with her dark eyes and shining hair and when she smiled she revealed the beauty of her brilliant, white teeth. She was curious and friendly and eyed Emma's pretty dressing-gown with frank admiration.

'I'm being spoilt,' Emma remarked as she sat up. 'I didn't expect to have tea.'

'Miss Aimee says all English people like tea in the morning and afternoon.'

'You speak English well. What is your name?'

'Cassandra but I'm always called Cassie.'

'I like that. Do you live at Belle Rive?'

'No. I come from the village. Mr Randell drove over very early this morning and asked if I would work at the house. He said that Esmeralda is too old and it wasn't fair to expect her to do the extra work.'

Emma frowned. 'Won't she be annoyed at the arrangement?'

'She will have to put up with it. Don't be afraid of her! She will not dare to harm you if I'm in the house.'

Noticing that Cassie was fingering the crucifix which was on a silver chain around her neck, Emma asked curiously, 'Are you a Catholic?'

'Yes. Miss Aimee says I have to look after you and see you come to no harm.'

Emma was startled for it seemed as if Aimee was expecting trouble. Steve must have told her what had happened the night before, hence the haste to get Cassie in the house.

She asked cautiously, 'What do you think you could do?'

'My faith will protect us. The old witch's power is useless when I wear my cross.'

Emma smiled. 'You are a good girl, Cassie. Thank you for explaining.'

She sighed after the girl had left her feeling uneasy and rather puzzled. I wish I could feel as confident as Cassie, she thought. Her faith makes me feel ashamed.

Aimee had told her the previous day to leave her letters on the bureau so that Steve could take them into Roseau to post. She saw that they had gone when she went in to

56

have breakfast and supposed that Steve had taken them early that morning.

'Can I help?' she asked brightly as she went into the kitchen.

Aimee shook her head. She looked very attractive in her pink candy-striped dress with her smooth, black hair tied back with a ribbon.

'There's nothing much to do unless you want a big breakfast,' she explained.

'I never eat much in the morning.'

'How about grapefruit, toast, coffee or tea?'

'Just right.' Emma smiled. 'Have you had yours?'

'No. I was waiting for you. Shall we have it in here?'

Emma nodded her head. 'Cassie is a sweet girl isn't she?'

'Yes. I remember when she was born. I was six then and couldn't understand why my mother was so distressed. I understood later on. It was because her parents weren't married.' Aimee smiled. 'It's usual here. Most of the islanders consider the marriage ceremony unnecessary. It took time and much persuasion to get Cassie's parents to agree to be married.'

'Are most of the villagers Roman Catholic?'

'Our villagers are but there are Methodist churches in other villages.'

'I would have thought their religion would have persuaded them to think marriage proper.'

Aimee chuckled. 'It's made no difference. One reason is that most Dominicans can't afford it. Some save and marry years after. My father used to say that it was because many years ago when they were slaves they weren't allowed to marry.'

'Aren't the women afraid when they have children?'

'On the contrary. Children to them means security for their old age. I have noticed that men with property tend to marry but even then they live together first.'

'How do you feel about it? Will you marry one day?'

Aimee's smooth oval face lost all its brightness. 'I was nearly married once,' she said sadly. 'Aunt Sophie broke it up and Benjie went away from the island.'

'I am sorry. Didn't she think he was suitable?'

'She said I was too young. It was two years ago. She spoke to Benjie's parents. I don't know what she told them but it was bad enough to make them all leave. I've not seen him since and he's not written.'

'When your father died did your aunt move in here and take over?'

'No. She stayed in Roseau. Uncle wasn't well enough to cope. She put Armand and his wife here to manage the estate.'

Emma finished her grapefruit then asked, 'What made him leave?'

'Steve was responsible for that.'

'Where did he come from? How did you meet him?'

Aimee laughed as she poured out the coffee. 'I first met Steve when my parents were alive. It was before the hurricane came. He was one of a Canadian team of foresters who came to carry out a survey. When they had finished they decided to do some sightseeing before they went back. They had left Trafalgar Falls and were on their way to the Boiling Lake. It lies deep in the jungle in the Valley of Desolation. It's really a geyser and it's a dangerous place to explore.'

Emma nodded. 'Someone I met on the plane told me about it. He said the gases lift the water to over six feet.'

'Yes. It looks as if it's bubbling. It's very impressive. Well, Steve and his friends never reached Desolation Valley because they were caught in a tropical storm. We do have some extremely severe ones. Luckily they came across Belle Rive and took shelter with us.

59

They stayed for over a week and I got to know Steve well.'

'Did he return to Canada?'

'Yes. I didn't think I would see him again. Then one day about a year ago he drove over from Roseau. He was astonished when he saw the new house. I explained all that had happened. He had two friends with him; a young man and his sister. Both had blond hair and the girl was very pretty.'

'Did he say why he had returned to Dominica?' Emma asked.

'His two friends, Ellis and Brenda, had come over to work in the Government offices. Steve said that he happened to have nothing going at the time and decided to take a vacation. I think that when he returned to Canada he felt restless. He has travelled about the world for most of his adult life.'

'What made him stay here?'

'I'm sure he had no intention of doing so. I asked them all to stay to lunch. It turned out to be a catastrophe. Armand came in very drunk — he used to be over-fond of the rum bottle — and his wife was unpleasant and served up a terrible meal. When I remembered how hospitable my parents had been I felt so ashamed.'

'Did Steve and his friends say anything

about it?'

'Not then they were too polite. But when Steve walked into the kitchen and found Armand's wife hitting me across the face he became very angry. A terrific row started and Steve warned Armand that he would report him and his wife to the authorities if he continued to get drunk and allow his wife to hit me.'

'Did it make any difference?' Emma asked.

Aimee smiled. 'It was so fortunate that Steve turned up when he did. I had had a miserable existence since my father died. Armand didn't wait for Steve to report him. He must have become frightened for that night when Steve and his friends had gone Armand and his wife packed their things and went. I haven't seen them since.'

'Did Steve suggest he take Armand's place?'

'He was very upset when he called in a couple of days later because he thought he had put me in an awkward situation. I asked him to stay and help me run the estate. He seemed reluctant at first then offered to stay until another manager could be hired. I think Brenda was the reason he made up his mind so quickly. If he stayed on the island he would be able to keep in contact with her. I could see he liked her.'

'I wonder why the Guidas didn't employ someone else,' Emma said thoughtfully.

'It was difficult for them because they were so far away. They accepted Steve after he had written to them and explained about the Armands. I know Aunt Sophie doesn't trust him because she sent those two women to spy on us.'

Emma cast a startled look at her. 'Is that why you think I was sent?'

Aimee was silent for a minute or two then said gravely, 'At first I thought so but now I think I was mistaken.'

Emma sighed. 'I'm so glad. I would hate to be taken for a spy. If your aunt had asked me to do that I would have refused to have come.'

Steve did not come in for lunch and Emma found the day dragged a little. She helped Cassie with the dusting, washed the lunch dishes then spent the afternoon roaming about the grounds around the house. It was mostly short, coarse grass with tropical shrubs and trees and she was delighted when she discovered a stream with clear crystal water where she could dabble her feet.

Changing from her slacks into a dress before dinner that evening Emma wondered what really had caused Steve to stay at Belle

Rive. It was not a very exciting job for a roamer to have and was highly different to forestry. Perhaps he's keen on Aimee, she thought then decided that was unlikely if Brenda was his girl friend. She must be the reason, she mused then began to speculate about why he had stayed so long. A year was a long time to persuade a girl to marry him. Perhaps he's not ready for that yet, she thought. All the same it does seem rather strange. It's obvious that Aimee likes Steve and she's come to rely on him.

Her brown silk dress high-lighted the golden tints in her eyes and she knew that it suited her. She was surprised that she was looking forward to meeting Steve again and told herself that it was because she had had rather a dull day.

Steve was sitting in the living-room when she went in. He had changed into white trousers and a casual open-necked shirt. His face and neck looked very sun-tanned against the white of his collar and his eyes seemed extremely blue as he stared frankly at Emma.

'Do you always look so good or are you trying to make an impression?' he drawled with a tinge of mockery in his voice.

She recovered swiftly from this unexpected banter, 'I haven't found it necessary to try,' she replied lightly.

'Conceited as well! I guess you are used to male flattery.'

'So familiar with it that I don't even notice.'

Aimee who had come from the kitchen and overheard, laughed. 'You've met your match, Steve. How does it feel?'

He grinned. 'I guess she's damaged my ego.'

'It will do you good. Women fall for you too easily.'

'I'm real pleased to hear that. I hadn't noticed.'

'Do you want some help, Aimee?' Emma asked ignoring Steve and following the girl into the kitchen.

'You could take the plates in. I put them in the oven to warm.'

'Where's Esmeralda?' Emma asked as she took a cloth and opened the oven.

'She's gone to some meeting or other. She won't be with us tonight.'

'I suppose Cassie has gone back to her village.'

'Yes. Steve thought she ought to help in the house now that you are here.'

'Cassie seems to think I need protecting.' Emma chuckled. 'She was certain that nothing could harm me if she was near.'

Aimee looked at her gravely. 'There is some truth in that. Cassie is a devout Catholic. Non-believers are a little frightened of her.'

'You are referring to Esmeralda aren't you?'

Aimee frowned. 'She can be troublesome. I didn't want you to be upset. Yesterday I noticed her antagonism.'

'You are very kind. It's good to know someone else noticed it.'

When they returned to Steve he remarked caustically, 'You've been a long time. I never had to wait for my meals before Emma came.'

All three passed a pleasant evening. Esmeralda's absence seemed to have relieved the tension which had been so noticeable the evening before. When Emma went to bed she was feeling more relaxed and happy than she had felt since she arrived.

The next morning when Emma turned up for breakfast she was surprised to find that Steve was still in the house. He was sitting reading an old newspaper and looked slightly impatient.

'Tell Aimee to buck up,' he said. 'Don't keep her talking.'

Emma nodded her head and went through to the kitchen. 'Are you going somewhere?'

she asked the Dominican girl. 'Steve seems to think I might hold you up.'

Aimee laughed. 'He's eager to get off. The mobile library calls in at the village today. He likes to go with me.'

'Can't you drive yourself?'

'Yes, I do sometimes.'

'I can take you if Steve wants to get on with his work. In fact I would like to come.'

'Don't spoil Steve's day. You remember the Canadian girl I mentioned? A few months ago she quit her government job and became a mobile librarian.'

Emma smiled. 'I see. Steve takes you so that he can have an excuse to see her. He must be keen.'

'I imagine so.' Aimee poured coffee into Emma's cup. 'He's a secretive man. It's difficult to know what he is thinking.'

Emma munched her toast thoughtfully. 'Does he meet Brenda in Roseau very often?' she asked when she had swallowed a mouthful.

'He goes into town a lot so I expect he sees Brenda and her brother. They are very good friends. I really will have to hurry. Steve doesn't like waiting. I will have to leave the dishes until I return.'

'Don't worry. I can do them or Cassie will.'

'I thought you were coming with us?'

Emma shook her head. 'I will be in the way.'

'Don't be silly! You can help me choose my books.'

Steve did not seem too pleased when Aimee told him that Emma was going with them. 'We shall have to use the land-rover then,' he said irritably. 'The back of the jeep is full of tools.'

'Don't bother,' Emma said quickly. 'You go without me.'

'Don't start an argument! You know real well you will come. We've wasted enough time already,' Steve drawled.

'Take no notice,' Aimee whispered as they followed him outside. 'Something has annoyed him. I find it best to ignore him when he's grumpy.'

The mobile library was parked just outside the tiny village and judging by the crowd of women and children surrounding the unit, it was extremely busy. The doors of the van were open and a pure black woman in an orange and white striped dress was supervising and keeping the chattering women in line.

As Emma walked towards them with Aimee and Steve she noticed the blonde, Canadian girl almost at once. She was neatly dressed in slacks and a vivid green blouse and was sitting on a stool date-stamping the books which had been selected. She raised her head and waved her hand at Steve and his two companions then went on with her task.

Aimee was right, Emma thought. She is quite lovely and how brown she is! When Brenda stood up and pushed her way towards them, Emma could see why Steve was attracted to her. She was confident and mature, direct in her dealings with other people.

'Real nice to see you Steve . . . Aimee,' the girl drawled giving Emma a darting glance from her bright green eyes. She smiled and held out her hand. 'You are the girl Steve had to meet, I guess. Are you interested in books?'

'Yes, very,' Emma replied as she shook hands. 'Do you go all over the island?'

'Only to the main villages.'

'It sounds interesting. I expect you prefer it to working in an office.'

Brenda chuckled. 'Sometimes. It's not too good after a downpour of rain. But it's not so boring and I do learn more about the island.'

Aimee touched Emma's arm. 'I ought to choose my books and return these,' she said with a glance at the volumes she was carrying. 'Do you want to come with me?'

Emma nodded and followed her through the crowd of women to the back of the van. She glanced back once and saw that Steve and Brenda had moved away and were deep in conversation.

She felt vaguely disturbed. Brenda was as sharp as a bird with her alert, bright eyes which seemed to miss nothing. Then Aimee was asking Emma's advice and she soon became engrossed in the books offered for loan.

No one hurried. The librarian was used to women changing their minds. Emma soon became accustomed to the noise and enjoyed listening to the local patois which was a mixture of old French and pidgin English. She could not understand a word of it although she listened carefully. But the gestures and friendly laughter served to keep her interested.

The Negro girl was stamping the books now because Brenda had not returned. Emma wondered what Steve and the Canadian girl were talking about for they seemed unaware of anyone else.

'Come and meet Cassie's mother,' Aimee said when they had finished with the van. 'She lives in one of the shanties.'

The village may well have been unhygienic but it was very pretty with its winding dirt road that had water running in an open channel down one side. The shacks, packed tightly together, almost hidden by trees and flowering shrubs or vines were constructed of wood with shuttered windows and all had galvanized iron roofs.

Shooing the chickens away from the path Aimee led the way into one of these shanties. Rather surprised, because it all looked so primitive, Emma noticed that it was wired for electricity. They entered an outside kitchen and came across a middle-aged woman who was cooking over the low wood fire. Aimee spoke to her in English because Emma was with her.

'How are you, Cleo?' she asked. 'I've brought Miss Fielder to see you.'

The woman straightened, wiped her hands on her apron and gave Emma an enthusiastic handshake. 'Cassie spoke of you. I'm real pleased to meet you. I hope my daughter is behaving herself.'

Emma smiled. 'She has been very good. I expect you are proud of her.'

The slim Dominican woman nodded. She looked gay in her red dress and white apron with gold rings dangling from her ears.

'Would you care for a drink?' she asked

hospitably.

'Thanks but we can't stay,' Aimee told her. 'Mr Randell is waiting to drive us back.'

Cleo said awkwardly, 'If Esmeralda is giving you trouble I don't mind having her here. I can keep an eye on her and her black magic nonsense doesn't worry my husband.'

Aimee shook her head. 'I promised my father I would look after her. You have enough family as it is.'

'One day we might be given a new stone house outside Roseau,' Cleo said tossing her dark head proudly. 'My husband works for the council now and they have promised.'

Emma noticed that there was a tap in the kitchen but the sink was a primitive one, very low and small. She thought it a miracle that anyone could use it without suffering from continual back-ache. She spoke about it after they had left Cleo.

'Most of the owners of the shanties have access to the same standpipe,' Aimee explained. 'Cleo was very excited when she had water piped to her house. There's a stream close by but no proper sanitation. It is not the same in all villages. Some have been improved.'

'They all seem very happy,' Emma remarked as they began to stroll back.

'There is plenty of work and they eat well. The children go to school and we are not too far from Roseau for the health clinics. Some remote places have problems for there are very few doctors.'

'They are packing up the books,' Emma said as they came in sight of the van.

'Yes. Steve is waving to us. He is impatient this morning!'

Evidently he had said good-bye to Brenda for he was sitting in the land-rover ready to drive off. The Canadian girl smiled at them as they passed.

'What is the matter, Steve?' Aimee asked after they had left the village behind them. 'Are you annoyed with us?'

'No. I didn't want to bother you but I guess you will have to know sometime.' He changed gear noisily and without his usual care. 'Last night someone uprooted all the seedlings sent by the Banana Growers' Association. I felt so mad because it was an entire day wasted.'

'You can get some more, Steve. Why would anyone want to do that?'

'It's wanton destruction,' he said savagely. 'I can only think that it has been done to annoy me.'

Aimee asked carefully, 'Have you fired anyone recently?'

'No. I thought of that. Brenda told me that Armand has been seen in Roseau.'

'He must have done it,' Aimee said emphatically. 'He wants the estate to fail so that he can blame it on you.'

'Perhaps.'

Steve did not say much after that. He dropped the two girls off at the house and drove away immediately.

'Steve usually has lunch with me after I've been to the mobile library,' Aimee said. 'I've never seen him so cross.'

'It's understandable,' Emma said. 'He will have to do all the planting again.'

Cassie had prepared the lunch for them so they were able to sit down as soon as they got in. Esmeralda had not eaten with them since that first night and Emma, although relieved at her absence, felt a little worried. She did not like to think that she was keeping the old woman from her home.

After lunch they sat out in the sunshine until a sudden heavy fall of rain drove them inside. Emma wondered how Steve was faring but supposed he was used to the rain by now.

'It won't last long,' Aimee said with a light laugh as she shook the rain from her skirt. 'They say we have more rain than anywhere on earth.'

'I suppose that's why there are so many trees and it's so green,' Emma commented.

'I've been thinking about those banana seedlings,' Aimee said seriously. 'Esmeralda didn't come home last night and I haven't seen her today.'

Emma stared at her. 'You think she did it?'

'It's possible. She could have frightened someone and made them do it.'

'But why?'

'Because she felt spiteful. She's annoyed because we got Cassie here.'

Emma looked distressed. 'I hope that's not right. I feel I'm responsible.'

'Don't worry. She'll get over it. She's had her own way too long. I'm not going to think about it any more. It's time I started on the dinner. It's rabbit tonight and it will take a lot of preparation.'

Chapter Four

Steve was finishing his breakfast when Emma went into the kitchen the next morning. He looked tired but more inclined to be friendly. The evening before he had come in late and been rather disagreeable.

'Good morning, Steve,' Emma said brightly after she had spoken to Aimee. 'I don't usually see you at breakfast.'

'This is only your third morning! Does it seem longer?'

'Yes. Is that good or bad?'

'I wouldn't know.' He pushed his plate away and poured himself another cup of coffee. 'I was kinda rough on you yesterday. It was nothing personal.'

Emma smiled. 'I didn't mind. I knew you were worried. Did you get a fresh supply of seedlings?'

'I did. Some have been planted already.'

'I thought bananas went on growing year after year.'

'They do but sometimes we clear the land and use it for other crops. It's a small estate. I have to watch the price index. Bananas keep pretty steady but time is real important. They have to be shipped out quickly.' His gaze lingered on her interested face. 'You're a real copper-nob aren't you? Even your eyes have golden glints.'

'I was hoping I'd outgrown that. I like to think of myself as auburn.'

He grinned. 'You reckon you've suffered enough. It depends which way the light strikes. This morning it's red-gold and I can see a few tiny freckles.'

'Stop teasing her, Steve,' Aimee said sharply. 'I wouldn't stand for it, Emma. You look very nice.'

Steve's blue eyes looked hurt. 'Can't a guy give a girl a compliment without having it taken the wrong way?'

'We don't trust you,' Aimee said with a light laugh. 'Are you going to use the jeep today?'

'I guess so. Why?' he asked looking at her suspiciously.

'Emma said she can drive so I thought we might take a trip into Roseau. The land-rover would be more comfortable.'

'Sure, you take it. I prefer the jeep anyway.'

'That's marvellous,' Emma exclaimed

looking pleased. 'There's someone I ought to see there.'

Steve's eyes narrowed. 'The man I saw you with at the airport?'

'Yes. I promised to let him know how I was faring.'

'You needn't look so excited. He wasn't all that wonderful,' he drawled.

Golden sparks lit Emma's brown eyes but she kept her voice under control. 'He was very kind to me. Looks aren't everything.'

He grinned. 'There's hope for me then.' He stood up looking very tall and big. 'I'm off. Have a pleasant day girls.'

When he had gone Emma glanced at Aimee and smiled. 'I'm never sure when he's serious. He will keep giving me sly digs.'

'It's just his way,' Aimee said carelessly. 'I take no notice. He soon tires of his teasing.'

Both girls changed into summer dresses before they went. It was the beginning of April back home but here one took little notice of the seasons because the temperature only fluctuated between warm and hot.

'It will be hot and fairly dry until May,' Aimee explained when Emma asked her if they had summer and winter. 'June to October it's hot and wet and we have the odd hurricane. But we are lucky because we do not get nearly as many as the other

Caribbean islands. But we do have more tropical storms and they can do a lot of damage.'

Emma smiled as she started the car and drove off. 'It's the price you pay for your good weather. One thing, you don't have to worry over much about clothes.'

'Sometimes I wish we did. When I look at the glossy magazines I become envious.'

'We all do. The average girl can't afford to dress like a model.'

'You have some pretty things,' Aimee said. 'Would you mind if I had one of your dresses copied?'

'I would be flattered. Have you a good dressmaker?'

'Cassie's mother would make it for me. She's very clever with her hands.'

'I wish I had been able to bring a few more things with me but that's the drawback when you travel by plane.' Emma laughed. 'Another steep incline! I'd never get fined for speeding here.'

'Some people say it's hillier than Switzerland.'

Emma overtook a bus, the first one she had seen. The one at the airport had looked more like a car. This one was an open air truck with fitted benches.

'We haven't far to go now,' Aimee remarked. 'Slow down when you reach the top of this hill. You will be able to see a lovely view of Roseau and the sea.'

'It's much larger than I thought it would be,' Emma exclaimed as she pulled into the side of the road and cast a glance at the sparkling ocean and town beneath them.

'It's our capital and like most cities it gets larger every year. That's the roadstead beyond where you can see the ships.'

'There's only one thing that disappoints me about Dominica,' Emma remarked as she drove on. 'I haven't seen any golden beaches with waving palms.'

'Foreigners mistake us for the Dominican Republique. We do have one or two beaches where you can bathe but most of them are dark and look dirty. To the north the cliffs overhang the sea. Swimming is dangerous. The Atlantic waves pound into the bays. It's very beautiful where the mountains rise sheer from the sea. I suppose you can't have everything.'

It took them some time to cross the Roseau river because of the heavy traffic but once they gained the town centre Emma was able to relax and take in her surroundings.

She was charmed by the grey, wooden houses with their balconies and shuttered windows. Even here where modern and old buildings mingled there were open water-courses in the streets. Aimee explained that it was the only way to deal with the sudden torrential storms. Built on a plateau south of the town centre were the public buildings and churches including a Cathedral and Government House.

'Would you prefer to find your friend first?' Aimee asked after they had parked the car.

'He said he was staying at the Fort Young Hotel,' Emma said.

'That's the eighteenth-century fort over-looking the harbour. It's been turned into an hotel. We can walk there. It will give you a chance to see the city.'

Emma thought it quite impressive. A hill towered behind the Cathedral and palms shaded the broad sidewalks where people loitered to gaze into the store windows.

They did not have to enquire for Gerald Forbes at the hotel. Emma and Aimee found him at the bar close to the pool in the charming court-yard of the hotel. He seemed very pleased to see them and in-sisted that they have a drink with him.

'You were lucky to catch me,' he said after they had seated themselves at a table. 'I'm due at the lime estate at two o'clock.' He glanced at Aimee. 'You grow limes at Belle Rive, I believe.'

'Yes. We sell them to your firm.'

'Do you expect a good crop this year?'

'About the same as usual. You will have to ask my manager.'

'Steve Randell? Yes, I've met him.' He turned to smile at Emma. 'You are enjoying your stay?'

'Very much. When do you have to go back to London?'

'In three or four weeks. I was intending to drive over and see you but I wasn't sure whether you would like that.'

'Please come,' Aimee said eagerly. 'I love to have visitors. What about having lunch with us one day?'

'It will have to be next week. Would Tuesday be all right?'

'How will you get there?' Emma asked.

Gerald smiled. 'I've hired a car to get me around. I have to visit various parts of the island and some of the estates are in remote places.'

They finished their drinks and Gerald went into the hotel to have an early lunch. He had asked the girls to keep him company but they had refused giving shopping the excuse.

'He seemed very disappointed that we

didn't lunch with him,' Aimee remarked as they strolled back to the centre of the city. 'I suppose we ought to have accepted. His hotel is one of the best in town. All the rooms have baths and are air-conditioned.'

'I would liked to have had a swim,' Emma said. 'The pool looked so inviting. Gerald is lucky. He told me he comes over twice a year.'

'He's a charming man. You ought to encourage him then he will want to see you when you go back to England.'

'I expect he has his own circle of friends.'

'I could see he liked you and he seemed very anxious about you.'

Emma did not want to discuss Gerald Forbes. She knew that he was attracted to her but she did not like him enough to encourage him. Now I've met Steve he seems so ordinary, she thought. Oh dear, I'm being awfully unfair. I ought not to compare them. Steve is a loner. I would be crazy to imagine anything could flare up between us. He's a hard-bitten adventurer and I know very little about him.

Aimee was excited at the thought of having someone else to lunch. She made out a menu daily, constantly changing the different courses until Emma became bored with listening to her. It seemed a very long week and she was relieved when the day actually arrived. I do hope Gerald has remembered, she thought. Aimee will be terribly disappointed if he doesn't turn up. Steve must be as fed up as I am with listening to Aimee's chatter about the lunch.

At breakfast that morning Steve said carelessly, 'Now that the great day has arrived are you feeling nervous, Aimee?'

'No, of course not. You are coming in to lunch today, I hope.'

'I wouldn't miss it for anything,' he drawled.

Emma was surprised when Aimee told her that Steve would be coming back to lunch with them. Perhaps he wants to discuss the lime crop with Gerald, she thought. I wouldn't have thought he would have bothered. But when Gerald drove in with Brenda she naturally assumed that she was the reason Steve had decided to join them.

'I hope you don't mind, Aimee,' Brenda said. 'When I heard Gerald was coming over here I couldn't resist the chance to visit Belle Rive. It's my free day.'

'Do you know each other?' Emma asked in surprise.

Brenda and Gerald exchanged a glance of amusement.

'All the whites know each other,' Brenda

drawled. 'There's only a hundred or so on the island and every newcomer is noticed. We get invited to the same parties. Gerald and I met at my former boss's house.'

Gerald smiled at her. 'Brenda took pity on me. I'm not much of a bridge-player so she kept me company.'

The Canadian girl chuckled. 'I've been well rewarded; two delicious dinners! Have you seen Fort Young, Emma?'

'Yes. Aimee and I had a drink there with Gerald.'

'It has a real good *boutique* if you ever need anything up to date. I've been here so long now that I have to rely on the local fashions.'

'The dress you have on isn't out of date,' Emma said as she glanced at the green flowing skirt and low neckline. 'I bought a similar one a few weeks before I came here.'

'That's comforting. I like to keep up a standard.' She gave Gerald a coquettish glance with her bright green eyes. 'Does it suit me, Gerald? Do you approve of it?'

He chuckled. 'I'm no judge of women's clothes. You and Emma look very sophisticated but Aimee surpasses you both.'

Emma smiled to herself. She thought that Gerald had got out of that very tactfully.

Aimee was wearing a white lace blouse

with a full red skirt. She looked gay and excited, not the least bit nervous that she had to serve a lunch that she had prepared. Emma envied her confidence.

'Are you going to wait for Steve?' she asked knowing that the meal was ready and that it would spoil if kept much longer.

'No. He's so unreliable. He won't mind if we start without him. There's only two courses. I decided to keep it simple.'

Emma chuckled when she thought of all those agonizing indecisions but she kept her amusement to herself. 'It smells delicious!' she exclaimed. 'Do you want me to take it in?'

'No. I will do that. Would you pour out the wine?'

Brenda sniffed and wrinkled her nose when Aimee put the steaming dish on the table. '*Callaloo!* Aimee you're a magician. I adore crab stew the way you Dominicans cook it.'

Emma had not tasted it before but she soon had to agree. It was wonderful. All three were eating it with enjoyment when Steve walked in.

'Sorry I'm late,' he drawled apologetically. 'I will scrub some of the dirt off before I join you.'

Emma was bringing a hot plate in for him

when he returned and was conscious of his eyes appraising her white dress. It was simply but cleverly tailored to fit her slim figure to advantage.

'The girls look real nice,' he drawled as he sat down next to Brenda with Emma facing him. 'I feel out of place in my working togs.'

Gerald said pleasantly, 'You won't notice that when you've tasted Aimee's *callaloo*.'

Steve grinned. 'We are well acquainted. Aimee knows it's my favourite.'

Brenda said gaily, 'You're spoilt. Now I know why you've stayed so long.'

'Aimee's taught me a few things,' Emma remarked giving the girl a friendly smile.

'I might test you on that,' Gerald said lightly. 'When you return to London you can invite me to a home-cooked meal.'

Emma glanced at him curiously. 'Do you have to cater for yourself?' she asked.

'Yes. I have a small bachelor flat. Usually I find it more convenient to eat out.'

Emma noticed that Steve was looking glum and asked him quietly, 'Has the food got cold? Would you like me to heat it up?'

'No, it's okay. I will have some wine if you have finished.'

'I will get it,' Brenda said quickly. Her heady, cloying perfume wafted across to Emma when she moved. This was a different young woman to the one they had met at the mobile library, Emma thought. Then she had been friendly and casual. Today she was kittenish, ultra-fashionable and feminine.

Fruit sundaes followed then coffee which they took outside to drink. It had been very warm all morning and it was pleasant sitting in the shade and chatting amicably. Steve said very little seemingly content to relax and listen to the others. But Brenda became restless. Gerald was fixing his attention on Emma and she thought that Aimee and herself were being neglected.

'I'm going for a stroll,' she said and stood up. 'Come on, Steve a walk will do you good.'

'Is that a fact!' Steve smiled lazily. 'I can do with a rest. You're too energetic, Brenda. The sun is at its peak. You're asking for trouble.'

She frowned and sat down. 'You're not being very sociable today.'

Emma said diplomatically, 'I'm going to help Cassie with the dishes. You will have to entertain Gerald and Steve, Brenda.'

'I told Cassie to leave them,' Aimee said. 'I will come with you.'

On their way into the house Emma remarked, 'I've noticed you don't like Cassie washing the dishes. I thought today you might have made an exception.'

'She's too heavy-handed with china. She has cleared the table and tidied the room. I sent her into town to do some shopping for me.'

'Did she mind? It's such a long way to the bus.'

Aimee laughed. 'You worry too much about people. I employ Cassie. She has to do what I tell her.'

Emma felt surprised. Brenda was not the only one she was seeing in a different light. Did Aimee think like that about herself? she wondered. Her aunt is paying me to stay here. So far Aimee has treated me politely and generously. But now I can sense a deep-rooted contempt for those who serve her. Perhaps my instinct is warning me to be on my guard. I'm sure I didn't imagine it.

She was rather quiet as she washed the dishes. Aimee glanced at her once or twice with an amused smile on her oval face.

'You are silly to allow Brenda to upset you,' she said. 'She's jealous of you. Can't you see that?'

Emma gave her a startled look. 'You're wrong, Aimee. I never gave her a thought. Why on earth would she be jealous of me!'

'She's used to having the men's attention.

Gerald made it obvious he's more interested in you. It annoyed her.'

Emma laughed. 'That's ridiculous! She doesn't strike me as that type of girl. Anyway you said Steve is fond of her.'

'He is but that doesn't prevent her from flirting with other men.'

'You speak as if you know her very well. Does she come here often?'

'She's been to lunch with her brother. He spoils her too. Ellis and Steve go out of their way to please her.'

Emma dried her hands then said carefully, 'Don't you like Brenda?'

'I don't dislike her. I resent her. She has all that attention lavished on her and I have nothing. It is unfair.'

Emma gazed at her compassionately. 'I'm sorry. I had forgotten about your young man. I can understand you feeling resentful.'

Aimee sniffed and put her handkerchief to her eyes. 'I try not to think about him then when I see Brenda and Steve together it reminds me. I tell myself that if Benjie had really loved me he would have come to see me and find out for himself whether it was true what my aunt said.'

'You have such courage, Aimee. You are pretty, confident and intelligent. Someone else will want to marry you.'

The girl's eyes brightened. 'Yes. That is what I tell myself. You have made me feel better, Emma. It's such a lovely day. Shall we go out somewhere?'

'I don't mind. Where do you suggest?'

'You haven't seen the Botanical Gardens. It's near Roseau so Gerald and Brenda won't have far to go afterwards.'

'I don't mind seeing it again,' Gerald said when Aimee suggested that they all go there. 'It's interesting as well as beautiful. It's the best in the West Indies and is a centre for important agricultural and forest research.'

'Count me out,' Steve grunted. 'I do enough foot slogging on the estate. Anyway I ought to get back. If I don't keep an eye on the men they will start on the rum bottle and nothing will be done.'

Brenda looked cross. 'It's only for one afternoon! You might have asked me if I wanted you to go.'

'We've been there several times. Gerald will look after you.'

Aimee said carelessly, 'We can take you home first if you don't want to come, Brenda.'

'I didn't say that,' the girl said quickly.

Steve raised an eyebrow, smiled crookedly at Emma and strode across to the jeep. He gave the impression that he was bored with the lot of them and Emma found herself being irritated by his lordly casualness.

'Take Emma in your car, Gerald,' Aimee said. 'Brenda can keep me company.' She knew that this would annoy the Canadian girl but did not care. Brenda had been an uninvited guest and she was not going to have her spoil Emma's day.

Steve had climbed into the jeep but had not driven off. He was watching with a cynical smile twisting his mouth. When he saw Emma climb into Gerald's car, he scowled and clenched his fingers over the wheel. They waved as they passed him but he made no sign that he had noticed and waited until they were out of sight before he drove off.

Once outside the Botanical Gardens it was easy for Emma to slip away from Gerald. Brenda attached herself to him and stayed close for the rest of their stay there. As Emma was genuinely interested in the marvellous array of tropical plants, shrubs and trees in their splendid setting, she preferred to have Aimee's company for the girl could tell her the names of the various species.

'It's five o'clock,' Gerald said as they all paused on a tiny bridge which spanned a rushing stream. 'What about coming back to the water-front with me and having a snack at the Green Parrot?'

'Sure, why not,' Brenda said eagerly.

Emma glanced at Aimee who shook her head. 'I can't. I have Steve's meal to prepare. You go if you want to, Emma.'

'Someone would have to bring me home,' she said doubtfully. 'I will come back with you.'

'That's no problem,' Gerald exclaimed. 'I can run you home.'

Seeing that Emma was hesitating, Brenda said impatiently, 'Come on, Gerald. Can't you see that she doesn't want to come.'

If she hadn't said that Emma would have gone with Aimee. But Brenda was beginning to irritate her. 'I will come, Gerald,' she said.

'Good!' His eyes brightened. 'We might as well make a night of it. Instead of a snack we can have an early dinner and then go on to the club to listen to the steel band.'

Emma could not help being amused at Gerald's tactics. On reaching the hotel he took them to the bar and introduced them to a young man whom he was acquainted with. Obviously he had made up his mind that he was not going to have two young women on his hands for the entire evening. Emma wondered which one he was going to plant on Victor Hemmings, the unsuspecting young man. She was not left in doubt for long.

'Brenda used to work in the Government Offices, Victor,' Gerald remarked. 'How about joining us for dinner?'

'Thanks. I would like that.' Victor smiled at Brenda uncertainly. He pushed his spectacles up then fingered his tie nervously. 'Brenda and I have met before.'

Because the girl was making no attempt to put him at his ease, Emma felt sorry for him. And when Gerald left them to book a table she began to draw Victor into the conversation. But when Gerald returned to take them into dinner she had to leave the young man to get on with Brenda as best he could.

'Gerald might have asked me before he invited Victor,' Brenda said crossly when she and Emma went to the cloakroom after they had finished dinner. 'I used to work with him. He's a real ninny. None of the girls could stand him. He's the last man I'd want to date.'

'I'm sorry,' Emma said. 'It's lucky that you don't have to be alone with him.'

'He will expect to take me back to my hotel,' Brenda replied in an annoyed voice.

'Have you always lived in the hotel? Don't

you find it expensive?'

'Not really. It's only small. I stay there because the food is good and it's clean. They make deductions when I eat out.' She chuckled. 'Now you can understand why I angle for invitations.'

Emma laughed. 'I would do the same. Meals can be expensive.'

The evening was not a great success. Emma thought afterwards that only she had enjoyed it. It was a new experience for her to listen to the calypso and steel bands. But the others tired of it and Gerald took them back to his hotel for a last drink.

The last person Emma had expected to see was Steve and her eyes widened with astonishment when she saw him standing at the bar.

'What brings you here?' Gerald asked. 'Did you change your mind and decide to come?'

Steve shook his head. 'I've only just come in. I guessed you would come back for a drink. I can save you the trouble of driving Emma home.'

Gerald frowned. 'I was looking forward to it.'

'That's too bad,' Steve drawled. 'It's a real tricky road to Belle Rive especially at night.'

Gerald said stiffly, 'I'm well used to driving at night. Emma would have been quite safe.'

'It is a long way,' Emma sensing unpleasantness between the two men intervened quickly. 'It is rather late and you would have to drive back, Gerald. It would be early morning before you reached the hotel.'

Brenda chuckled. 'He's well used to that. After a night club or party we often arrive home when the city is waking up.'

'I prefer to feel fresh in the mornings,' Victor said with a smile. 'Shall we make a move, Brenda?'

Emma saw Brenda glance at Steve and wondered what she was thinking. Not very pleasant things she imagined. Surely Steve ought to have offered to take Brenda back to her hotel. I would be very annoyed, she thought, to know that he had driven into town to take another girl home.

She felt very awkward as she watched Brenda and Victor move away from the bar. Gerald was glaring at Steve as if he wished him anywhere but there. Emma was apprehensive fearing a quarrel. She sympathized with Gerald for it was his evening after all. First it had been spoiled by Brenda and now Steve had turned up.

She glanced at Gerald and gave him a warm smile, 'It's been a lovely evening.

Thank you so much.'

He said anxiously, 'Aren't you going to have a drink before you go?'

'No. Steve has finished his and I do feel rather tired.'

'I shall see you again before I go back?'

'I will look forward to it.'

Steve nodded to Gerald and followed Emma out of the hotel. She was feeling a little annoyed with him so did not speak until they reached the land-rover.

'Why did you really come?' she asked quietly. 'You knew Gerald would take me home.'

'I felt like a drive.' He opened the car door. 'Get in and stop looking so cross.'

'I feel annoyed. You spoilt Gerald's evening.'

'He will get over it. You ought to be grateful.'

'What for?' she asked in surprise as he took his seat.

He started the car and grinned at her before he drove off. 'Don't tell me you enjoyed this evening? I guess I wanted to save you the embarrassment of being driven home by him.'

'He's very kind and pleasant. Why don't you like him?'

'I reckon I won't answer that. You're not

in a very good mood.'

'If I wasn't cross before I am now after that remark!'

'If we are going to quarrel all the way I shall regret coming,' he said. 'I thought I was doing you a favour.'

She remained silent until they had crossed the bridge and had gained the outskirts of the town. Her annoyance had ebbed by then and she found that she was actually enjoying the prospect of being with him.

'It's pleasant driving at night,' she remarked. 'What a gorgeous moon!'

'This is the first time we've had any time together since that first day when I met you,' Steve drawled.

She laughed. 'We see each other every day!'

'Aimee is always there. Are you really going to see that stuffed shirt when you return to London?'

'I wish you wouldn't talk about Gerald like that!'

'Okay, don't get riled. I guess I'm peeved because he has all the opportunities.'

'Do you wish you hadn't taken over the estate?' she asked in an attempt to take his mind off Gerald.

He turned his head to give her a brief

stare. 'Whatever made you suddenly ask that?'

'It doesn't seem your kind of scene. It's a lonely job and responsible.'

He smiled. 'I bet you have an entirely wrong picture of me. You think I'm a bum out for what I can get?'

'No!' she sounded horrified. 'Aimee told me how you helped her. I think it was very generous of you to give up your time for her.'

'I owed it to her folks. I felt sorry for the kid. But I must admit that just lately I've been having a few doubts. I can't see how the deuce I'm going to extricate myself from Belle Rive.'

'Because Aimee has become so dependent on you?'

'Yes, that's one of the reasons.'

'I've noticed that you haven't been too happy lately.'

'That's something, I guess. That you noticed, I mean. The estate takes up too much of my time. I would have enjoyed taking you around, showing you some of the beauty spots.'

'With Brenda you mean.'

'Sure if that's how you'd prefer it. She's a real nice girl. I'm real pleased you get on. You scared of being alone with me?'

'That's not what I meant.'

'I can't make you out. I've never found girls difficult to get on with before.'

Emma remained silent. He was negotiating some dangerous twists in the road and she did not want to distract his attention. Some of the trees made grotesque figures in the moonlight and she was thankful that she was not driving.

'Have you always been a drifter?' she asked idly when the road had widened.

'I don't like the sound of that but I guess it's basically correct. I left home when I was eighteen.'

'What caused you to do that?'

'A girl.' He chuckled. 'I met her a few years back and wondered how I could have been such a fool.'

'Tastes do change. Did you regret leaving home?'

'No. I was raised on a ranch. It was a pleasant but narrow life. I wanted more than it could offer. Now I reckon I ought to go back. It's time I settled down.'

'What will you do?'

'Go back to Manitoba and take over my ranch. When Pa died he left it to me. I'm the only son.'

'Is your mother alive?'

'No. I guess I wouldn't have left if she had been.'

'You amaze me! Fancy taking on Belle Rive when you have a ranch of your own!'

'Daft isn't it? That's what happens when sentiment takes over.'

'Who is looking after your ranch?'

'My brother-in-law. I offered to help him get a place of his own if he would run my outfit for a couple of years. The time limit is up this June. I shall have to go back then.'

'Does Aimee know?'

'Not yet. I've been intending to tell her but it's not easy.'

'I can well believe that. You ought to tell the Guidas.'

'A month's notice will do for them.'

Emma had been so engrossed in what he had been saying that she had not realized that they were drawing near to the house. Steve switched off the engine then climbed out and walked round to open the door for Emma.

'Thanks for the lift,' she said lightly and began to move away.

He reached out and caught her by the shoulders twisting her round to face him. Then crushing her against him he kissed her hard on the mouth.

'I wish you hadn't done that!' she exclaimed shakily.

'You didn't want me to?' he asked with a note of incredulity in his deep voice.

'No!' She was certain that he could hear the loud beating of her heart as he stared at her intently. His fingers pressed into her shoulder-blades and she was aware of a melting sensation which needed an effort to control.

His hold loosened and his arms fell from her. She looked sweet and vulnerable with the moonlight on her red-gold hair, her brown eyes soft and bewildered.

'Go in, Emma,' he said abruptly.

She stared at him uncertainly for a second or two then turned and ran towards the house. As she did so a figure in white moved from one of the unshuttered windows. Emma did not notice. She was dazed with mingled joy, fear and anger.

If she had glanced back she might have wondered why Steve was taking so long to follow her. He was leaning against the car his lean face taut and unsmiling. He stayed there until he saw Emma's light go on in her room then moved slowly towards the house.

CHAPTER FIVE

Steve had gone when Emma awoke the next morning. Cassie innocently informed her of the fact when she brought in her tea. Emma's instant reaction was one of relief. It would give her more time to pull herself together before she saw him again.

After what had happened last night she could no longer pretend to herself that she did not care for him. The realization frightened her. He couldn't possibly care for her. He knew that she would not be there long. That kiss had meant nothing more than a pleasant flirtation.

She found herself becoming angry when she thought of Brenda. He obviously had some affection for the girl. They treat each other familiarly as if they are very close, close enough to trust one another, she thought. It was unfair of Steve to make a pass at me. She sighed. I expect I'm making too much of it. It didn't mean anything and it's foolish of me to dwell on it. We have to live in the same house. I shall have to behave as if it was of no consequence.

Aimee said little at breakfast but afterwards she seemed unduly inquisitive about what had happened. Emma, not wanting to discuss other people's affairs, answered her as briefly as possible.

'Did Steve and Brenda have a quarrel last night?' Aimee asked as she cleaned the surface of the stove.

'No. They didn't see one another for long,' Emma replied.

'I thought they might have because Steve was so angry when he left here.'

'I can't think why he should be cross.'

'He came in later than usual and wanted to know where you were. Then when I told him that Brenda had gone with Gerald and you to Roseau he got very red in the face. He hardly spoke to me at dinner and went out soon afterwards. I guessed he was going to find Brenda.'

That might explain Steve's behaviour, Emma thought. He could have been trying to hit back at Brenda. Yet I wouldn't have believed that he would act like that. I suppose if Brenda has been fooling about with other men he might behave out of character. But why would he be angry about her going out with Gerald and me? Perhaps he wasn't angry at all just fed up. Aimee doesn't understand. He's not so wrapped up in his job as she imagines.

Emma decided not to bother about it. Nothing much had happened and as far as she knew Brenda and Steve were as friendly as ever. She had something else on her mind. She had been at Belle Rive over two weeks now and had not had any replies to her letters. The Guidas might be waiting for her to write again as she had not said very much but she was very surprised that her mother had not written. If I have not heard by the end of the week I will write to her again, she told herself worriedly. It's very peculiar that I haven't received any mail.

The next two days were not very happy ones for Emma. Steve went out in the morning before she was up and did not have dinner with them. As she and Aimee were out in the afternoon each day they missed him when he came in to change before going out. Was he deliberately avoiding her, Emma wondered. Was he annoyed or was it only embarrassment? The latter she found difficult to believe. Steve was not easily disconcerted.

'Steve's having trouble with Brenda,' Aimee said on the second night at dinner. 'I do wish she would hurry up and make up her mind. Steve gets so irritable when he's quarrelled with Brenda.'

'Did he say he was meeting Brenda?' Emma asked for some times she wondered whether Aimee made things up. She always looked as if she was secretly amused when she talked about Brenda and Steve.

'He wouldn't go to Roseau for any other reason. But he did drop a hint or two. No man likes to discuss his tiffs. But he did show me the present he had bought for her.'

'He must have forgiven her then,' Emma said carelessly and went on to talk of other things.

The next evening Steve was in for dinner. Emma noticed that he was looking pleased with himself and was annoyed with herself for feeling depressed and uneasy. Obviously he had not been worrying about the evening he had driven her home and she felt a little foolish that she had thought he was avoiding her. She caught him watching her once or twice during dinner and tried to affect a carefree air. Not very successfully she found when he spoke to her after they had finished the meal.

'What brings you here?' Gerald asked. 'You look as if someone has promised you a new coat and given you hankies instead.'

She laughed for his good humour was infectious. 'I didn't realize I looked so glum.'

'Are you getting bored with living here?'

She shook her head. 'I'm a little worried, that's all. I haven't heard from home and I'm wondering if everything is all right.'

'Is that all! You've only been here three weeks.'

'I wrote the first day. My mother would be certain to reply right away.' She glanced at him enquiringly, 'You did post my letters?'

'No. Was I supposed to?'

'Aimee said you would if I put them on the bureau.'

He frowned. 'When was this?'

'The day I arrived. The next day they were gone so I thought you had posted them.'

'The only mail I've posted has been Aimee's and my own. I didn't see any of yours.'

Aimee laughed. 'I expect you picked them up without looking at them,' she said. 'You are always in a hurry.'

'I usually glance at them. I'm going into Roseau tomorrow and will call in for the mail. There may be some for you, Emma. I wouldn't worry.'

'Isn't no news supposed to be good news?' Aimee smiled. 'My aunt must be satisfied.

Evidently you told her what she wanted to know.'

Emma frowned. 'I said very little that's why I'm so surprised she didn't write.' She paused then went on, 'I haven't seen Esmeralda in the house for days. I've been meaning to ask you about her but keep forgetting.'

'She moved out soon after Cassie came to work for me.'

'I hope it wasn't because of me.'

'You didn't have anything to do with it. She's scared of Cassie or to put it more precisely she's apprehensive of her faith. She won't look at Cassie's crucifix and puts her hand over her eyes when the girl is close to her.'

'Cassie wouldn't have been asked to come if I hadn't arrived,' Emma said.

'You did Aimee a good turn,' Steve drawled. 'I've suggested several times that she ought to get rid of the woman.'

Aimee looked distressed. 'I feel responsible for her.'

'She has other places she can live. She made you feel real gloomy. Cassie is young and bright. There's a different atmosphere in the house.'

'Yes, I do agree about that,' Aimee replied. 'My mother couldn't stand her and only put up with her because of Dad. When I

107

think back I believe it was because he was superstitious. He told us that he wanted her here to look after me but I'm pretty sure it was because he was afraid to tell her to go.'

'She wouldn't harm you would she?' Emma asked curiously.

'No. She's fond of me. She's too old to change now. She's living with her sister who is about the same age as herself. They get on well so I expect she is happier.'

Steve laughed. 'I doubt whether she knows the meaning of the word.'

'She enjoys life in her way,' Aimee told him seriously. 'She gets satisfaction by being gloomy.'

Emma smiled. 'I can believe that! I've met people who like being miserable. It sounds strange but it is a fact.'

'What do you two do with yourselves all day?' Steve asked as he helped himself to a second cup of coffee.

Aimee winked at Emma. 'That's a typical male remark. If you really want to know, Steve, the day flies by. We have the house to look after and the meals to get. Emma takes me into Roseau some times to shop. We walk to the village and back or go for strolls not too far from the house. Sometimes we read in the afternoons if it's too hot to walk. And once or twice we've been swimming in the pool near the village.'

Steve frowned. 'Not the one the villagers use?'

'No. I'm not that stupid.'

'All the streams and rivers have such clear water,' Emma remarked. 'It seems strange when so many people use them. The women do their washing and shampoo their hair in them and one day I saw a man washing his car in one.'

'The streams tumble down from the mountains,' Steve said. 'They flow swiftly towards the sea. That's why they look so clear. But there is pollution near the villages. Do be careful. Never drink the water.'

Emma chuckled. 'I have enough imagination not to do that!'

Some of the emptiness Emma had been living with for the last few days had vanished and she was conscious of a sensation of well-being. It's only because you've seen Steve, she warned herself as she prepared for bed. Nothing has changed. You are only here for a few more weeks. Steve will go to Canada and you will return home. All the same it was good to know that they were back on their friendly footing, she thought. He's not annoyed with me and I don't think he was staying away because of me.

The next evening she dressed with more

care than usual choosing a long skirt and a frilly, white blouse which made her look very feminine. She looked in the mirror and eyed herself critically. Her skin, smooth and clear had tanned to a lovely golden colour. I don't look too bad, she thought, in spite of the few extra freckles. I knew I would get those. I always do when I'm in the sun. She sighed. Men always prefer blondes. However well I look Brenda will always outshine me.

She laughed and turned away from the mirror. I never thought I could ever be jealous, she reflected. Being in love certainly alters a girl. I'm not nearly as confident as I was. I hate to think of Steve and Brenda together. Are they really in love? Aimee says they are and I suppose she ought to know. It's stupid of me to doubt her. I shall get hurt if I hope for a miracle to happen.

Emma pulled the bead curtain aside and eyed the empty living-room disappointedly. Steve had not come in yet. Perhaps he was not going to join them that evening.

When she heard the sound of the jeep her heart began to race and she cautioned herself to remain still until her thoughts were under control. He came in looking big and strong and very dependable.

More relaxed now she asked with a faint smile, 'Had a busy day?'

'Not bad. You going somewhere?'

'Only to Belle Rive for dinner.'

'It won't do you justice.' He was pulling something from his back pocket. 'There were a couple for you in the mail. I guess you would like them now.'

'Thanks.' She took the letters and glanced at them eagerly. 'One is from the Guidas, the other from my mother.'

Aimee came from the kitchen and exclaimed, 'You're not ready, Steve! Do get a move on.' She glanced at Emma and said sharply, 'Will you come and help me? There's a lot of dishing up to do.'

Emma thrust the letters into the pocket of her skirt and followed the girl into the kitchen. Aimee usually preferred to see to the last details herself so her request for help from Emma came as a surprise especially when there did not seem much to do. And now that she thought of it Aimee had been behaving in a neurotic manner lately. She never wants me to be alone with Steve, Emma reflected. I can't think why unless she's jealous and is in love with Steve herself. But why me? Why not Brenda? She shrugged her shoulders. I'm being too introspective, she thought. There's probably nothing in it at all. Aimee and I are alone together far too much. We are bound to get on each other's nerves.

'Is everything okay at home?' Steve asked when Emma returned from helping with the dishes after dinner was finished.

'I haven't read them properly but I've gathered that neither my mother nor the Guidas have had letters from me. Your aunt sounds annoyed with me, Aimee. I think you ought to read it.'

Aimee scanned the letter quickly then handed it to Steve. He frowned as he gave it back to Emma.

'I reckon it's just as well she never got your letter,' he said curtly, his blue eyes glinting with anger. 'She did send you to spy on us.'

Emma glanced at Aimee who was looking at her doubtfully. 'If she did I wasn't aware of it,' Emma said defensively. 'She asked me to stay with Aimee as a companion. I know she was upset because the Armands had gone. I thought it was natural for her to be worried. Until I came here I didn't know the ins and outs of the estate.'

'She seems very anxious to know what Steve is like,' Aimee remarked. 'Why doesn't she come here and find out for herself?'

Looking at Steve and Aimee's serious faces Emma felt very disturbed. 'Perhaps your aunt will return now. I'm sorry you find it difficult to believe me. The only solution is for me to go.'

Aimee glanced at Steve. 'What do you think?'

'I'm inclined to believe Emma. I would be sorry to see her go.'

'That's what I thought. Stay until the beginning of June, Emma. By then we ought to know what my aunt intends to do.'

'She will send someone to replace me, I imagine.'

Aimee frowned. 'Aunt Sophie is a nuisance! Steve and I don't want anyone.'

Steve smiled. 'I can't stay here forever, Aimee. I shall be moving on at the end of May.'

'You can't, Steve! What about me? I shall be lost without you.' Aimee's face crumpled up and tears came to her eyes.

'You've always known I would leave one day,' he said kindly. 'I would leave now but for something important I have to attend to.'

'You are hoping to take someone back with you,' Aimee said shrewdly. 'I suppose I'm lucky that you have stayed this long.'

'I haven't regretted helping you out. I've written to your aunt and explained the position. She will find another manager.'

Aimee asked carefully, 'If this person

refuses to go with you, will you stay?'

Steve frowned. 'It's possible. It all depends on what the circumstances are.'

Aimee's face brightened. 'Let's not talk about it. It hasn't happened yet. A lot can happen in a month.'

Steve glanced at her doubtfully. 'Sure, if that's what you want. To get back to Emma's letters, it's strange that they didn't arrive at their destination.'

'I can understand one getting lost, but three seems too much of a coincidence,' Emma exclaimed.

'I'm sure they weren't with the other mail,' Steve said.

She said quickly, 'I wasn't accusing you.'

He smiled twistedly. 'I wouldn't blame you if you were. We both have come under a cloud. Misunderstandings can appear so easily.'

'Esmeralda was in the house then,' Aimee said worriedly.

Emma looked startled. 'Why would she take them?'

'She knew that my aunt had sent you. She would be afraid that you were sending a report to her.'

'I hope you don't think that. It would be a horrible thing to do. I wouldn't have come if they had asked me to do that.'

'They were hoping you would,' Steve said. 'They picked the wrong girl, luckily.'

She sent him a grateful glance. 'Thanks. I couldn't stay if I thought you didn't believe me.'

Aimee said angrily, 'Considering the estate belongs to me, Aunt Sophie has a frightful nerve. Steve, couldn't I do something about establishing my claim? It seems so unfair having to answer to the Guidas all the time.'

He said cautiously, 'They may have documents. Your solicitor told you to wait.'

'I asked him if my father left a Will and he said he didn't. So, as far as I can see I ought to inherit.'

'It does look like it.' Steve smiled. 'You will soon be twenty-one. It will all be cleared up then, I guess.'

Aimee said wistfully, 'If you were here I wouldn't mind not owning it.'

Steve said hurriedly, 'We decided not to talk about that. Do buck up, Aimee! I sometimes think you ought not to live here. You ought to have more friends.'

'Yes,' her eyes brightened. 'Away from here we would be happy.'

'I have things to do,' he said abruptly. He gave Emma a brief glance as he got to his feet. 'See you at breakfast.'

After he had gone Aimee's dark eyes

flashed as she exclaimed, 'He is too good for Brenda. How can she fool about with his friends when she knows how much he cares for her.'

Emma said flatly, 'I feel awfully tired. I think I will go to bed.'

'I thought you didn't seem yourself. All this has been upsetting for you.'

Emma shook her head. 'I feel relieved now that I've heard from home.'

'Would you like to go to the cinema tomorrow? There's an afternoon performance. It's easier to get in then. There's always queues a mile long for the evening performance.'

That's the disconcerting thing about Aimee, Emma thought. Just when we get to the brink of disagreement and uneasiness she does something kind or thoughtful. She makes me feel regretful and ungrateful. She's like a child trying to make up for some unpleasantness. I never know where I am with her.

'It would make a change,' she replied making an effort to look pleased although in her confused state she did not much care what she did.

I ought not to have agreed to stay, she told herself feeling very troubled as she parted the bead curtain and walked down the corridor. Even seeing the light beneath Steve's door hurt for it reminded her of his physical nearness. *He only wants me to stay because of Aimee,* she thought sadly. *He has his life all mapped out and it doesn't include me.* She felt forlorn and miserable as she got ready for bed. Every little tender incident between Steve and herself returned to plague her and she had a restless night in consequence.

Aimee and Emma set off soon after eleven o'clock the next morning. Aimee wanted to show Emma the covered market and planned to have lunch out to give them both a change.

'Brenda doesn't come to Belle Rive very often,' Emma remarked as she drove carefully over the winding, dipping roads. 'When does Steve manage to see her?'

'He used to go into Roseau most evenings but lately it's only been once or twice a week. I expect he sees her on her free day and afternoon. We don't see him in the day much. He could drop in at the villages she calls at.' Aimee chuckled. 'Lovers always find time to see each other.'

'Brenda likes to dine out and go to clubs. I suppose that's why she prefers Steve to go to Roseau.'

'I'm glad she doesn't come to see us,' Aimee said candidly. 'She's a nice girl but I never feel at ease in her company. I always think she's criticizing me.'

'You're too sensitive,' Emma told her. 'That's because you don't meet many people. You are a marvellous hostess, Aimee. You ought to entertain more.'

'That's exactly what Steve says. He's always telling me what a good cook I am. The way to a man's heart is through his stomach, at least that is what my mother used to say.' Aimee laughed. 'Steve would miss me. Don't you agree?'

'I'm sure he will,' Emma frowned to herself as she accelerated to take a steep hill. Steve's announcement that he was leaving Belle Rive had shaken Aimee more than a little. The girl seemed to be eagerly searching for excuses to keep him there. She is very attached to him, Emma thought worriedly. Every time she mentions him her face glows. I don't envy Steve when it's time for him to leave.

They were near the outskirts of the city when Aimee said brightly, 'We used to have an open market near the roadstead but now they have moved it to the other end of town. There's a very big covered market. People who have small-holdings bring their provisions in to sell on the stalls in the open part.

There's fish, meat and vegetables and fruit and lots of other things. I'm sure you will think it exciting.'

They spent a very pleasant hour strolling about, buying a few things and watching the people haggling over their wares. Emma was intrigued and amused at the traditional way some of the dark-skinned women were carrying their provisions; balanced on top of their heads. One woman even had a stem of bananas weighing her down.

'It's all a matter of balance,' Aimee said. 'It leaves their arms free and distributes the weight evenly. If you go to the ports you will see women loading the small boats which shuttle back and forth to the big ships. The Dominican women prefer to carry loads on their heads and most of them are barefoot.'

They ran into Gerald Forbes in the centre of the town and he insisted that they lunch with him. He did not take them to his hotel, choosing one that was nearer this time.

Emma chose crayfish and heart of palm salad for it was too hot to eat anything substantial. She had bought a white straw hat off one of the stalls in the market and looked charming beneath the shade of its wide brim.

'I wish I hadn't got to go back,' Gerald

said regretfully, his hazel eyes reflecting his admiration.

'Are you leaving soon, then?' Emma asked.

'In a couple of days.' He hesitated then went on, 'I have to drive over to Layou Flats tomorrow. I suppose you wouldn't care to come with me?'

Emma was just about to make some excuse when Aimee said blithely, 'You ought to go, Emma. The Layou is one of our largest rivers and it flows through a magnificent gorge. There's a hotel near there where you can swim in one of the shady, deep pools. It's called Flats but it's really very hilly. It's so mountainous on the island that hills are considered Flats.'

Emma laughed. 'After that wonderful description how can I refuse!'

Gerald said seriously, 'It's certainly worth seeing. Emerald Pool and Fresh Water Lake are interesting also. I wish I had a few more days free to take you sight-seeing. Boiling Lake is terrific but it's a strenuous trip and takes lots of hard walking.'

'I'm quite content to visit Layou. Too many beautiful places bewilder me and I can never remember them clearly.'

'I'm sorry to hustle you, Emma but we really ought to go if we want to be in time

120

for the first performance,' Aimee reminded her.

'It's been wonderful seeing you so unexpectedly,' Gerald told Emma before he left them outside the cinema. 'I will call for you tomorrow morning about eight o'clock, if that's all right.'

'He's madly in love with you,' Aimee remarked as they joined the queue in front of the ticket office.

Emma frowned. 'I'm sure he isn't. He's just being friendly.'

'He couldn't keep his eyes off you.'

'I always feel wary of holiday romances. They rarely last. I would have to know a man longer than that before I was sure.'

Aimee nodded her head. 'It is safer. Steve and I have lived together for a year now. We know one another very well.'

Emma glanced at her with startled eyes. 'You have had someone with you. I thought he was interested in Brenda.'

'Yes, he is,' Aimee spoke carelessly. 'You never know what might happen. Soon he might get fed up with waiting for her to make up her mind.'

'I never realized you were serious about him,' Emma said thoughtfully.

'I haven't thrown myself at him. He likes me. I know that.'

'Perhaps not in the way you expect. Aimee, do be careful. I wouldn't like you to get hurt.'

'We are getting closer to the ticket office,' Aimee exclaimed. 'They usually show American films so I hope you enjoy it.'

The film was a long one and they were late getting back to Belle Rive. Steve had come in early and was pacing up and down outside the house. He looked agitated and greeted them irately.

'Where the deuce have you been?' he asked curtly as he strode across to the landrover and opened the door.

'Have you been anxious about us?' Aimee asked in surprise. 'We got stuck in a traffic jam on the bridge out of Roseau.'

'Why are you so late? You would have missed the traffic if you had returned earlier.'

'We went to the cinema.' Aimee chuckled. 'I know why you are cross. You're hungry and there's nothing ready.'

He frowned. 'There's cold chicken in the refrigerator. I could have had that. I was beginning to think something had happened to you. I noticed the car had gone. You could have had an accident.'

'We are back and all in one piece,' Aimee said smilingly. 'I will go in and see to the dinner. It won't take long.'

'Do you have many road accidents?' Emma asked curiously after the girl had left them.

Steve seemed disinclined to go into the house and she stayed with him sensing that it was more than a trifling anxiety that was making him look so disturbed. He had not changed from his working clothes and she wondered why he had not taken the opportunity to bath and shave.

He glanced at her briefly. 'It wasn't only a road accident I was thinking of.'

'Is something worrying you, Steve?'

'Not now.' He smiled as he ran his hand over his unshaven chin. 'You look so smart you are making me feel dishevelled. Where did you get the hat?'

'In the market.'

'It's cute and so is the blue dress. Where did you have lunch?'

'How did you know we went out to lunch?'

'I came back about one o'clock. Cassie told me you had gone out. She didn't know where.'

'I see. We had lunch at the Calabash.'

'Expensive place!'

She smiled. 'We didn't pay. Gerald treated us.'

Steve's blue eyes narrowed and his lean

face tightened. 'Why didn't you mention you were going to meet him?'

'We didn't know. We met him unexpectedly in town.'

'He's not letting the grass grow under his feet, is he?'

'It was kind of him to ask us to lunch,' Emma said sharply. 'I am acquainted with him.'

'I hadn't forgotten. Are you becoming serious about him?'

'I don't have to answer that. If you are going to be nasty I'm going in.' Turning her back on him she began to walk away.

'Emma!'

'Yes?' she replied glancing back.

'Come here.' He did not move and after a slight hesitation she walked back.

She felt surprised and uneasy as she noticed the nervous twitch at the corner of his mouth. 'There is something wrong! What is it, Steve?'

He shook his head, stared at her intently for a second or two, then spoke as if he was choosing his words with care. 'I'm not so busy these days. I thought we might take a picnic lunch to Trafalgar tomorrow. There are twin falls there which are real lovely. We could start early and have the entire day to ourselves.'

She was silent for so long that he moved forward and took hold of her hands, staring perplexedly at her downcast face. But when she shook him off his eyes glinted with anger.

'Did you take this long to make up your mind to lunch with Gerald?' he asked in tones of annoyance.

'No, of course not.'

'If you don't want to come say so and get it over,' he said bitterly.

'It's not that,' her brown eyes were distressed as she answered him. 'I would like to come but I can't. I've promised Gerald I would go with him to Layou tomorrow.'

'I see!' Steve hunched his broad shoulders and stepped back.

'I can't disappoint him. He's going home in two days.' Emma glanced at him uncertainly. 'Why don't you take Aimee? I'm sure she would go with you.'

'I can make my own dates,' he said stiffly. 'If the other guy is more important that's that.'

Emma stared at his angry retreating figure in uneasy amazement. Why was he so taut and belligerent? And how was she to know that he might want to take her out the next day? It was the first time he had suggested taking her out. Why didn't he take Brenda?

I suppose she's working, Emma thought. He fancies a day out and thought I would be available. He really is the most aggravating man! Perhaps it's just as well I can't go. If he's set on marrying Brenda, I would be foolish to spend a day with him.

She sighed as she followed him into the house. All the same, she told herself sadly, I would have enjoyed going with him. I'm not looking forward to a day's outing with Gerald.

Chapter Six

Steve waited to see her off the next morning, much to Emma's surprise. Gerald was only a few minutes late so they did not have long to talk alone. Aimee was in the kitchen and Emma and Steve strolled outside to enjoy the sunshine.

Emma was looking cool and neat in a sleeveless yellow dress and white sandals. She was conscious of uneasiness because Steve would keep staring at her. But when she realized that he was as nervous as she was she began to relax. He was trying to make amends for his angry behaviour the day before.

'You remind me of daffodils,' he said gruffly. 'I hope you will enjoy your day. Layou Gorge is beautiful; a place to remember.'

He caught his breath unprepared for the warmth of her smile. His blue eyes softened and his lips curved in response.

'Thank you, Steve,' Emma said gravely. 'Perhaps we could visit the Falls some other day.'

'Sure,' he drawled. 'I don't begrudge one day.'

She gave him a startled glance thinking it a strange remark. Then Gerald arrived and within a few minutes she was off.

'Did you know that the Caribbean sea was once a great inland lake?' Gerald asked as he drove northwards at a leisurely pace.

'How could it be a lake?'

'Because a chain of mountains stretched from Trinidad to Florida. When the sea broke through only the highest peaks remained. Dominica had the highest in the chain that's why it is more mountainous than the other islands.'

'It sounds fascinating. How do you know all this?'

'I've always thought Dominica was the most beautiful. I was interested enough to delve into its history. The highest mountain is Morne Diablotin in the north and, the Layou and Pagua rivers flow west and east from the valleys between Diablotin and Morne Trois in the south. If you can imagine a backbone of mountains running north to south with a flattish bit in the centre then you have it.'

'There's nowhere really flat is there?'

'Grand Savanna but that grassy plain was only caused by an overflow of lava. The mountains are volcanic you see.'

Emma chuckled. 'There's always a drawback.'

'There have been a few tremors but nothing serious lately.'

They did not talk much after that for Gerald had to concentrate on the hair-raising, winding road which was almost vertical at times. Emma, when she could summon enough courage to take her eyes from the steep ascent, turned her attention to the breath-taking views. She had never seen such a mass of tree ferns and palms, bamboo and mahogany, cedar and banana trees.

'Staggering, isn't it?' Gerald remarked with a grin. 'I ought to have borrowed Steve's jeep. We could have taken the Layou River road but I wanted you to see some of the interior.'

Altogether it was a wonderful day for Emma. Gerald was at his best, treating her with a care which was not too noticeable. He knew how to be attentive to women and Emma having resolved to enter into the spirit of the outing thoroughly enjoyed herself. They swam in the pool of the new hotel, had lunch and afterwards clambered over the rocks to see the magnificent gorge.

'I haven't enjoyed myself so much for ages,' Emma exclaimed as they prepared to drive back.

'It's not finished yet. After I have called in on my firm's clients we will go back to Roseau and have dinner.'

'I ought to go back to Belle Rive.'

'Don't spoil it. This is the last chance I shall have to be with you.'

'Have you seen Brenda lately?' Emma asked not wishing to argue about it.

Gerald laughed. 'I see her most days. As a matter of fact I saw her last night at a birthday party.'

'Has she mentioned that she might be leaving soon?'

'No. What makes you ask?'

'Steve will be leaving at the end of May.'

'You thought she would go with him? I know she's fond of him. You could be right. Brenda said she was going to Belle Rive today.' Gerald chuckled. 'I sensed Steve was jealous of me but I thought it was because of you.'

'I will accept your offer for dinner,' Emma said abruptly. If Brenda was at Belle Rive the later she returned the better. It would be too painful having to see Steve and Brenda together and having to listen to their plans for the future.

'I knew you would.' Gerald smiled at her warmly. 'It will be a perfect finish to a marvellous day.'

They had a drink at the bar before going into the hotel restaurant for dinner. It was a popular place and all the tables became occupied soon after they seated themselves.

They had nearly finished their meal when Gerald said curiously, 'Do you know that man over there? Don't turn round just look casually at the table to your left.'

Emma slid her glance to the table Gerald had mentioned and stiffened with shocked surprise. 'It's Señor Guida,' she said. 'He's my employer.'

'I was becoming annoyed with him. He's been casting furtive looks at you ever since we came in.'

'I wonder why he's here? I shall have to go over and speak to him.'

'You needn't bother. He's coming over to us.'

Señor Guida bowed and smiled at Emma and Gerald. 'Forgive the interruption. I waited until you had finished. I thought you had not noticed me. How are you Señorita Fielder?'

'I'm fine, thank you. I'm surprised to see you. Are you staying in this hotel?'

'No. My wife is not feeling well. She preferred a quieter place. We only arrived yesterday.'

'I am sorry. Please give her my regards.' Noticing that the Señor had been casting curious glances at her companion she hastened to introduce them.

'It is good to see that you are enjoying yourself,' Señor Guida said smoothly.

Emma did not think he meant that sincerely. She glanced at him uneasily wondering what he was really thinking. The small Spaniard could be very caustic when he was displeased.

'Have you been to Belle Rive yet?' she asked politely.

'No.' Señor Guida glanced quickly at Gerald then whispered to Emma. 'We need to have a serious talk but it is inconvenient here. Come to our Guest House tomorrow morning. Caribee House is not far from the centre of the town.'

'Very well. I will do that,' Emma told him.

He turned away then twisted back. 'I would rather you didn't mention that you have seen me,' he said softly.

Emma was thankful that he did not wait for a reply. She did not think that she could comply to his request. She felt that she owed Aimee and Steve some loyalty. They ought to know the Guidas had arrived on the island.

'Do you know that young woman he's with, Gerald?' she asked curiously, thinking that what Aimee had told her about her uncle might have a grain of truth in it. 'She's quite lovely.'

'I met her once. She's a beauty queen from a local village.'

Emma laughed. 'No wonder you don't want to go back! I've heard that every village has a beauty queen.'

'None so pretty as you, Emma,' Gerald said gallantly then in an eager voice added, 'If you are coming into town tomorrow you can have lunch with me, I won't be leaving until the evening.'

Emma looked doubtful. 'The Guidas might have plans for me.'

'Lunch won't take long.'

'All right. I don't suppose Señora Guida will mind. She's an understanding person.'

'It's getting late. I ought to drive you back.'

The restaurant had emptied and only the waiters were hovering in the background. Emma felt tired and subdued. Señor Guida's arrival had confused her and she sensed that it meant trouble for Aimee and Steve.

She was very quiet on the journey back to Belle Rive and Gerald glanced at her once or twice with a frown of disappointment on his thin face. She had been so gay all day; right up to the moment that darned Spaniard had spoken to her. Last time it was Steve who spoilt our evening, he mused. I seem to be unlucky. I never can get through to her. It's beginning to look as if I shall have to wait until she returns to London.

Steve had stayed up for her. He was sitting in an armchair reading, but threw the book aside when she went in.

'Had a good time?' he asked with a faint smile.

'Marvellous. The island is lovely.'

'Aimee left some soup in the oven for you.'

'That was kind of her but I don't feel hungry. I had dinner at Gerald's hotel. I will turn the oven off.'

'I can do that. You go off to bed. You look tired.'

'Yes. We did a lot of walking.' It was odd how easily they were talking to one another, she reflected as she answered him. It was as if they knew each other so well that there was no need for explanations.

Her reflections were short lived. 'Something has upset you,' Steve said abruptly.

Startled she glanced at him quickly. He was frowning and she found that she could not meet his keen blue eyes.

134

'No, there's nothing wrong,' she said flatly. 'Good night, Steve. I appreciate you waiting up for me but you needn't have bothered.'

His face hardened. 'I wouldn't have slept knowing you were out. These are dangerous parts. I would have done the same for Aimee.'

She left him then longing for the seclusion of her room. The brief spell of well-being had gone. Why didn't I tell him I had seen Señor Guida? she asked herself doubtfully. I suppose I didn't want to spoil the illusion he had created; sitting there waiting for me to come in as if he really cared what happened to me. She smiled sadly. Then he went and spoilt it by mentioning Aimee.

At breakfast the next morning Aimee wanted to know how the day's outing had gone and seemed more excited about it than Emma who was beginning to have misgivings regarding the Guidas. Aimee chattered so much that it was difficult to get a word in edgeways and she looked so happy that Emma put off giving her the bad news until they had eaten.

'Did Brenda come over?' she asked as she waited for her coffee.

'Yes. It was her afternoon off. How did you guess?'

'Gerald said she might. He met her at a

party the night before.'

'Steve was hanging about for most of the morning. He seemed all on edge. I was beginning to wonder what was wrong with him. Then when Brenda arrived I guessed he had been hoping she would come.'

'He wasn't expecting her,' Emma said thoughtlessly.

'Why are you so sure?' Aimee looked surprised.

'Just something he said. I expect I misunderstood,' Emma replied with an attempt to cover up.

'You must have. They went off for the afternoon. Steve came back alone just before dinner.'

'I'm sorry you were alone, Aimee.'

'I didn't mind. What's the matter, Emma? You look really fed up this morning.'

Emma smiled. 'I'm sorry. I suppose I shall have to tell you. When I was dining with Gerald last night I saw your uncle.'

Aimee gazed at her in shocked silence for a few moments then exclaimed, 'They've come back! Was Aunt Sophie with him?'

'No. He said she wasn't feeling well. They arrived the day before.'

'I suppose that's why they didn't come here.'

'He said they were staying at the Caribee.'

136

Aimee sighed. 'I wish they hadn't come back. They will start interfering in my life again.'

'Your uncle didn't want me to tell you but I thought you ought to know.'

'Yes, forewarned is forearmed. I don't trust either of them.'

'I have to go and see them this morning,' Emma said. 'Do you want to come with me?'

'That wouldn't be wise. You go and find out why they have come.'

'Señor Guida asked me to be early so I ought to go now.'

Aimee who had been frowning said thoughtfully, 'I'm not going to tell Steve yet.'

'He might ask you where I have gone.'

'I will make up some excuse.'

'I did promise to have lunch with Gerald afterwards.'

'Good! I can tell him that. He might decide to go over and see them. I think we ought to find out why they have come first.'

Emma nodded. 'It may be nothing much. If it is serious I will come back right away and let you know.'

'Don't break your lunch date. Even bad news can wait. I think they would have

137

come straight here if something had been wrong.'

Emma had chosen a simple golden-brown dress to wear for the visit thinking that she ought to appear more formally dressed. Señor Guida had left her with the impression that he had not approved of her dining out in the same hotel as himself.

She found the guest house quite easily and when she mentioned whom she wished to see was ushered into a medium sized lounge. Señora Guida was the only one in there. She was lying on a settee looking pale and strained.

'It is good to see you, Emma. You look very well.' The Dominican woman smiled and waved her hand towards a chair near her. 'Do sit down, child. I'm not going to eat you.'

Emma did as she was bid and glanced at her with concern in her brown eyes. 'You look ill. I do hope it's nothing serious. You were so fit when I last saw you.'

'It is nothing. Now I have seen you I will improve. I have been so worried. There was no letter from you. I didn't know what to think. I was afraid that you had left Belle Rive.'

'I'm so sorry, Señora. I did write the day I arrived, to you, my mother and a friend.

None of the letters got to their destination.'

The Señora frowned. 'Did you write again?'

'Yes, over a week ago. Apparently you didn't get that either.'

'No. That is why I have been so upset. It is very strange is it not?'

'Very. Someone didn't want you to get my letters. I thought Esmeralda had taken the first ones but she doesn't come to the house much now.'

Señora Guida swung her legs to the carpet and sat up straight. 'Are you saying that Esmeralda has left Belle Rive?'

'Yes, soon after I came. She lives with her sister now.'

'That is bad, very bad! Who is helping in the house?'

'Cassie.' Emma was startled at the way the woman had received the news of Esmeralda's departure and asked curiously, 'Do you think the old woman ought to have stayed?'

'Yes.' The Señora closed her eyes for a few seconds then opened them to stare at Emma doubtfully. 'I can see you do not agree. But it is serious. I wouldn't make a fuss about it if it wasn't. If I had known the old woman was not with my niece I would have returned sooner.'

'She seems such a frightening old woman,' Emma said looking puzzled.

'She is but she has been at Belle Rive a long time. She is very fond of Aimee. I cannot expect you to understand and I do not think this is the right moment to explain. Obviously you have enjoyed your stay so there is no immediate worry. Things have gone smoothly, no?'

'Yes. Aimee and I get on well. She is an intelligent girl.'

'That is so and that is why it is so unfortunate.'

Emma frowned. 'You are thinking of the estate? Aimee told me that there was some misunderstanding.'

The Señora shook her head. 'It is all quite legal and proper. I have never discussed the position with my niece so she has misinformed you. My husband and I will do what is best for her. It is a very sad situation. Please do not encourage Aimee to think that the estate can ever be hers.'

'She's not said a lot about it.' Emma was not quite sure what to say for she had only Aimee's account of what had happened when her father died.

Señora Guida's dark eyes brightened. 'That is good to hear. My niece has treated you well?'

'She has been very kind considering she didn't want another companion.'

'So, she told you about the others?' The woman stared at her thoughtfully. 'I made a mistake when I sent them. With you it has been different, I can see. Aimee is highly strung. It is not good that she be alone too much.'

'You have arranged for someone to take my place when I leave?'

The Señora shook her head. 'It will not be necessary. My husband and I will look after Aimee. What is your opinion of Mr Randell?'

Emma hesitated. How could she describe Steve's worth in one sentence?

'I believe he manages the estate well,' she said. 'Aimee likes him. He has been very good to her.'

Señora Guida's eyes narrowed. 'You think he is to be trusted? Has my niece conducted herself properly?'

'Yes. Mr Randell, Aimee and myself are all good friends.'

The woman nodded. 'His letters have been respectful. It is a pity he has decided to leave. If he had been willing to stay on we would not have considered selling the estate.'

Emma's eyes widened. 'Can you do that?

141

I mean hasn't Aimee got any claim at all?'

The Señora smiled sweetly at her. 'I commend your loyalty, child. You needn't be afraid that we shall rob Aimee. Her future is well looked after.'

'Is she to know who is going to buy it?'

'There's no secret about it. Armand has kept in touch with me since he left. He has been negotiating for us. A fruit grower's firm already established in Dominica has made a good offer for it. A Mr Forbes contacted Armand and negotiations are proceeding.'

Emma looked at her in astonishment. 'Gerald Forbes?'

'Yes. Do you know him?'

'I have met him.' Emma felt too flabbergasted to say any more.

'He's a reliable man isn't he?'

'I thought so,' Emma replied lamely.

'There is nothing to worry about then. Don't look so upset, my dear. I shall not expect you to leave before June. I feel a little exhausted so I won't keep you any longer.'

'Am I to tell Aimee that you are going to sell Belle Rive?'

Señora Guida frowned then shook her head. 'It would not be advisable, no. I would rather tell her myself. We shall have to come to some arrangement about the house. You can mention it to Mr Randell if you wish. I will leave that to you.'

'Do you intend coming over to see Aimee?'

'No. It would be better I think if she came to me. Ask Mr Randell to bring her over tomorrow morning. We can have a talk before lunch.'

Emma felt very disturbed and worried as she left the Caribee and returned to the land-rover. Aimee was not going to be very pleased when she received a summons to visit her aunt. And how was she going to react to the news her aunt would give her? Thank goodness I haven't got to break that to her, Emma thought. It will break her heart. Aimee's so sure she has a claim on the estate.

It was not until she was about to drive off that she remembered having promised Gerald to lunch with him. She glanced at her wrist-watch, saw that it was nearly one o'clock and switched off the engine. She climbed out reluctantly for Gerald was the last person she wanted to see right then.

He was waiting outside the Guest House when she returned there and greeted her warmly. 'I was afraid I had missed you,' he said. 'Where would you like to eat?'

'Somewhere near here. I can't stay long. I have to get back.'

He glanced at her curiously. 'You don't sound very enthusiastic. Aren't you pleased to see me?'

As she could not answer this truthfully she walked farther up the road and paused outside an hotel. 'They serve lunches here. Shall we go in?'

Gerald glanced at her perplexedly during the meal but kept his questions until they had nearly finished. 'You are annoyed with me about something,' he said. 'You might as well tell me.'

'The Guidas have made a deal with you haven't they?'

'Not exactly. Their former manager asked me if my firm would be interested in buying Belle Rive. I had to go along with it.'

'You pretended you didn't know Señor Guida the other evening.'

'I don't know him. The only person I've met regarding the deal is Armand.'

'I thought you were a person I could trust. Now it seems I was mistaken,' Emma said bitterly.

He glanced at her in alarm. 'Why are you so upset? My firm will pay a good price for it.'

'To whom? The Guidas? What about Aimee?'

Gerald frowned. 'I understood that the

property belonged to the Guidas.'

'That's what they say. Aimee believes differently. It was never split up after her grandfather died and her father took over.'

Gerald groaned. 'Another of those doubtful tenures! In my view they are best left alone.'

'You won't go ahead with it then?' Emma asked eagerly.

'It's out of my hands now. The firm's solicitor will deal with it. You needn't worry. If Aimee has a legal claim my firm will drop it.'

'She hasn't any documents apart from the deeds for the house. I do think you ought to have told us what you were up to.'

He laughed disbelievingly. 'You are making me out as a villain. My firm is always on the lookout for suitable properties. I had to pass the information on to them.'

'It was sly and underhand to do it without telling us at Belle Rive. You behaved as if you were a friend.'

'I leave my business affairs behind when I go out socially. I can't see I have done anything terrible.'

'It will cause Aimee much distress. It looks as if the Guidas want to sell it before their niece has a chance to do anything.'

'There's an easy way out of that,' Gerald

said sensibly. 'Tell Aimee to see her solicitor and get him to write to my firm and explain the position.'

'I can't do that. I've promised the Señora not to tell Aimee.'

Gerald smiled. 'Why get yourself involved in these people's problems. You aren't going to be here much longer.'

'It's easy for you to say that. I'm fond of Aimee. I wouldn't like to see her get hurt.'

Gerald gazed at her thoughtfully. 'The Guidas wouldn't attempt to sell Belle Rive if they weren't legally entitled to it. You can rely on my firm to act in a legal manner.'

'It all seems so unfair,' Emma exclaimed. 'How would you like it if after your father's death an aunt took over the estate you were sure was yours?'

Gerald shrugged his shoulders. 'Don't let this come between us. I can't do anything to help now. You will allow me to phone you when you return to London?'

'Very well,' she said reluctantly. She did not wish to part bad friends although at the moment she had no desire to see him again.

She hid her annoyance and talked of other things until it was time to go. Gerald seemed satisfied that they had cleared up their differences and left her in a more cheerful frame of mind.

Steve returned to the house for lunch. He had not said he would be in and Aimee glanced at him in surprise.

'I thought I was to be on my own,' she said. 'I haven't prepared much. Shall I make you an omelet?'

'Sure, anything will do!' He frowned and glanced around the room. 'Where's Emma? Has she gone for a swim?'

'She's lunching with Gerald.'

'Again!' He scowled. 'I thought she was supposed to be keeping you company.'

'Be fair, Steve. She's hardly had any time off since she came.'

'She had all day yesterday!'

'Don't be so grumpy! She will be back soon.'

He followed her into the kitchen. He looked annoyed and irritable and drummed his fingers against his chair.

'Does Emma talk to you about Forbes?' he asked abruptly.

'Emma never says much about herself. I'm sure she likes him. She wouldn't go out with him if she didn't. And it's obvious Gerald is attracted to her.'

'You're a great help!' he ejaculated angrily.

'There's no need to take your bad temper out on me,' Aimee said mildly. 'You will have to be patient.'

147

'I'm fast running out of that commodity,' he said bitterly. 'I'm not my own master any more. It's a deuce of a job living with uncertainty.'

'Would it help if we went out this afternoon?'

'No. I can't spare the time.' He raised his head and gave her an apologetic smile. 'Sorry I'm being such a bear. Thanks for offering.'

'You might feel happier if Emma went back sooner. You wouldn't have any uncertainty then.'

Steve looked grim. 'No, I wouldn't, would I?' he said tersely and got to his feet. He went through the door as if he was charging into a beast about to attack him and stormed his way out of the house.

Aimee forgot his ill-humour once he was out of sight and began to turn out the cupboards she had planned to clean. When Emma returned soon after four o'clock she had nearly finished and welcomed the chance to have a break.

'I will make some tea,' she said brightly then after a swift glance at Emma, exclaimed, 'Good gracious! What's the matter, Emma? You look like a tragedy queen!'

Emma laughed shortly. 'It's been a trying day. I will tell you in a minute. Right now I could do with that tea.'

Aimee glanced at her doubtfully as she went towards the kitchen. It could only be bad news for Emma to look as upset as that!

'Have my relations dismissed you?' she asked as she placed a cup of tea on the low table near Emma.

'No, nothing like that.' Emma smiled, sipped her tea for a few minutes then exclaimed, 'That's better! I felt so dry, Señora Guida asked me so many questions.'

'She would. I hope you told her nothing has happened here.'

Emma glanced at her doubtfully thinking it was a strange thing for her to say. 'I told her everything was all right,' she said.

'She is not going to interfere then?'

'Not with the present arrangement, no.'

Aimee was looking faintly disappointed. 'Why did you look so upset, then?'

'I'm sorry, Aimee. I didn't mean to alarm you. I have a slight headache, that's all.'

'Didn't my aunt give you any messages for me?'

'She wants Steve to take you to see her tomorrow morning.'

'I thought she might want to see Steve.' Aimee smiled. 'She's going to be surprised, isn't she? She will never believe I could get such a fine man.'

Emma cast a startled look at her bright face. 'For a manager you mean. Yes I imagine she will be pleased.'

'I wish she hadn't said tomorrow. I wanted to take my dress back to Cleo to be altered.'

'I can do that for you. We pinned in the alterations. I can tell Cleo how you want it done.'

'That's all right then.' Aimee's dark eyes shone. 'I think I'm going to enjoy tomorrow. It will be good to see Aunt Sophie's face when she sees Steve.'

Emma tried to hide her misgivings. She knew only too well that Aimee was in for a huge disappointment. It's just as well that Steve will be with her, she thought. It might be better if I could warn him what is in store but how and when? Aimee never leaves us together. Perhaps if I went out to meet him on his way back I could tell him briefly without Aimee knowing.

'Steve came in to lunch. He asked where you were and I told him you were lunching with Gerald. I think it's all settled between Steve and Brenda. He seemed in high spirits and could not stop talking about her.'

Emma said, suddenly making up her mind, 'I think I would like to leave at the end of next week, Aimee. It will only be a week sooner than we had planned. Now your aunt is here there's no point in staying on.'

Aimee's expression was guarded. 'If that's what you want, Emma. It is rather boring here.'

Emma had been waiting for her to protest and felt taken aback because she had received her suggestion amicably. Aimee had always given her to understand that she would be unwilling to part with her. Now it seemed she did not mind. Serves me right, Emma told herself wryly. I'm not as indispensable as I had imagined.

'When you see your aunt tomorrow would you tell her I've decided to leave?' Emma asked.

'Yes, she won't mind after she has seen Steve.'

Always, Steve, Emma thought. The girl is unable to think of anyone else. How is she going to exist after he has gone? She didn't seem to mind that Brenda had finally decided to marry Steve. I suppose it's because she lives in the present. She hasn't a great deal of imagination. It's very bewildering. And I feel very sorry for her. I thought I knew her but every now and then she does something or says something which astonishes me.

It was easier than she had thought it might

be to slip out of the house to meet Steve. Aimee was preparing the dinner and took little notice when Emma said she was going for a short stroll to ease her aching head.

It was nearly the time when Steve usually came home and Emma met him at the end of the grassy track which led up to the house. When he caught sight of her he pulled the jeep up smartly and climbed down.

'Hi!' he said giving her a brief smile. 'You look serious. Is something wrong?'

'I saw the Guidas this morning,' she said hurriedly.

'I didn't know they had come back!'

'Aimee didn't want you to know. I saw Señor Guida when I dined with Gerald.'

'I see. The Guidas asked you to go and see them. What did they want?'

'They told me that they are going to sell Belle Rive to Gerald's firm.'

She was expecting him to become angry but he appeared unmoved. His lean face looked tired and he gave her the impression that he was welcoming anything which would release him from the burden he had taken upon himself.

'You don't mind,' she said flatly.

'No. It had to end sometime. I've heard rumours. There's something queer about the whole set-up. I've had a few suspicions now and then.'

'What about?' Emma gazed at him in a puzzled fashion.

He smiled. 'When you look at me like that I want to comfort you. Don't look so worried, honey. It's not important.' He sighed. 'I'd like to bundle you into the jeep and drive away right now.'

'It's not as bad as that, is it?' she asked in alarm.

'Not to you evidently.' His lips smiled with an effort. 'From this clandestine meeting I gather you don't want Aimee to know her aunt's intentions.'

'Señora said I could tell you but she wanted to speak to her niece herself.'

'We should be thankful for small mercies. Aimee's not going to like it. I feel real sorry for the kid.'

'Can't you help her?'

'I will do what I can when I know the facts. Aimee's a little mixed up about the ownership of the estate.' Steve turned back to the jeep. 'Coming?' he asked briskly.

She shook her head and began to walk back to the house. Steve passed her and pulled up ahead of her. Then together they entered the house.

CHAPTER SEVEN

Emma awoke early the next morning even before Cassie came in with her tea. It was unusual for after a restless night she tended to fall into a heavy sleep when day was breaking.

I must have been tired, she thought as she glanced at her wrist-watch and saw that it was a few minutes to seven o'clock. I feel wonderfully refreshed. It's amazing what a few hours real sleep can do.

She swung herself off the bed and pushed the louvred shutters open. The sun felt warm on her bare arms and she leaned out to breathe in the salt-laden air. There was quite a keen breeze this morning and she could smell the sea.

It's going to be a glorious day, she mused as she glanced up at the deep blue sky. I've only got another week. I really ought to make the most of it. If Steve and Aimee are out all day I shall be able to please myself

154

what I do. I've been allowing my love for Steve to ruin my stay here. I've got to live without him when I go back so I might as well start now to be self reliant. The resolve did not console her but she did feel more resigned. I suppose I shall have this hollow feeling inside for months perhaps years, she told herself sadly. I shall never feel quite the same again and I shall never forget Steve or this lovely interlude. But I do have a wonderful memory to lock away in my heart.

You are getting morbid and sentimental, she told herself as she slipped into her dressing-gown and went across to the bathroom. If Steve has chosen Brenda then there's nothing to be soulful about. Other girls have the same problems and learn to overcome them.

As she had plenty of time she shampooed her hair and set it leaving it to dry naturally. When Cassie knocked on the door and came into the bedroom she was sitting by the window in the sun.

'Everyone's early this morning!' Cassie exclaimed as she gave Emma the tea. 'Miss Aimee is having breakfast with Mr Randell. I didn't expect to find you awake.'

'They are going into Roseau. I won't know what to do with myself. Can I give you a hand?' Emma said giving her a smile.

'If you like but there isn't much to do. Miss Aimee said you were to take anything you fancied from the refrigerator for your lunch.'

'It sounds as if they are going to be away all day. I can write some letters and this afternoon I shall go and see your mother about Aimee's dress.'

'The one she copied from your blue one? There's no need for you to go all the way over there. I can take it with me when I go.'

'That's kind of you Cassie but I have to tell your mother about the alterations. Will she be in after lunch?'

'Yes. She's going to Roseau this morning but she will be back by then.'

'How do your mother and Esmeralda get on?' she asked, suddenly thinking how lucky she was not to be left alone with the old woman.

'Not very well. Esmeralda has been making a nuisance of herself lately. She calls at any time and stays too long. My mother has to tell her to go because hints have no effect.'

'Does she want to come back here?'

'That's the strange thing. She says she never wants to come back. She's been prophesying evil things. She only believes in bad spirits and she gives them gifts.'

'Why doesn't she believe in good spirits?' Emma asked curiously.

Cassie chuckled. 'There would be no point. If they are good they will do no harm. The gifts are bribes to keep them from harming her.'

'What kind of gifts?'

Cassie's eyes fell beneath Emma's candid gaze. 'She makes sacrifices,' she said almost inaudibly.

'Animals you mean?' Emma was beginning to feel uneasy.

'Sometimes. There are people in the village who say she takes their children. No one has found any truth in that but it is a fact that some have disappeared.'

'She can't be as bad as that!' Emma exclaimed in a horrified voice.

Cassie looked solemn. 'You need not be frightened of her, Miss Emma. She's only been to the house once or twice since I've been here.'

Emma heard the land-rover start up as the girl finished speaking and turned to the window to watch. Steve with his usual impatience was urging Aimee to hurry up. She was laughing and took her time getting in. Emma waited until she saw the land-rover disappear amongst the palms before she turned back to Cassie.

'Miss Aimee is very excited,' Cassie said. 'She likes to be taken out.'

Cassie had spoken as if she was talking about a child and the thought struck Emma that it was not the first time she had done that. I must be imagining it, she told herself after Cassie had left her. It was all that reference to Esmeralda and evil spirits. I became quite alarmed at the way Cassie spoke of it.

Emma had breakfast, tidied the kitchen, then sat down in the living-room to write her letters. She decided to give Cassie a treat and invited her to lunch with her in the dining-room instead of eating as she usually did in the kitchen. Then remembering that Aimee did not like Cassie to wash the dishes, she did them herself before going to her room to change into a clean summer dress. If she had known what was in store for her she would have chosen slacks to protect her legs but perhaps it was better for her peace of mind that she could not see into the time that was stretching ahead.

She did not hurry for she had the rest of the afternoon to fill in. The hilly terrain made the muscles of her legs ache and she stopped when she came to a stream or reached the top of a hill so that she could admire the view as she rested.

The suspension bridge over a swiftly flowing stream had frightened her the first time she crossed it because it looked so narrow and frail. But she was used to it now and did not mind feeling it sway as she moved. She even paused in the centre to watch the sparkling water and to stare beyond the forested hills to the mountains where to her delight she saw a distant rainbow.

Today the village slumbered in hot sunshine. Even the laughter and chatter of the women was missing. Passing one of the closely-packed shacks she caught a glimpse of Esmeralda's tall form and averted her gaze to hurry by quickly.

Cleo greeted her enthusiastically and insisted on making tea for her. Emma would have preferred a long, cool drink but she did not say so for fear of offending the woman. The tea was very weak and Emma drank it sugarless thinking it would be more refreshing. She had become used to goat's milk and hardly noticed it now, although she guessed it was why Steve always preferred to drink coffee. It seemed less noticeable then.

'That was lovely, Cleo,' Emma said. 'It's very hot today isn't it?'

Cassie's mother nodded her head. 'It will get hotter. But the evenings are always cool. We notice the heat more here because we are in a valley.'

Emma unfolded the dress she had brought with her. She felt a little awkward when she pointed out the alterations for she had not thought them necessary.

'It's only a fraction out here and there,' Emma said. 'I would not have minded but Aimee is very particular.'

Cleo's eyes twinkled. 'Miss Aimee would not accept a garment without a slight alteration, on principle.'

'Don't you mind? You have done such an excellent copy.'

'Bless you, no, Miss Emma! I know why she does it. Maybe it's good for my character. She likes to show me she is the employer and she exercises her privilege.' She laughed. 'Sometimes I deliberately make a mistake so that she can complain.'

'Will it take you long? Aimee seems to be in a hurry for it.'

'No. I will do it tonight. Cassie can give it to her in the morning. Esmeralda was asking about you yesterday.'

'Does she blame me for making her leave Belle Rive?'

'She hasn't said anything. I think she is jealous of you.'

'Jealous?' Emma looked at her in surprise. 'I would have thought it would have been

Cassie she was jealous about.'

'No. It's because Aimee is friendly with you. Esmeralda is a stupid old woman. She thinks she is the only one who ought to look after Miss Aimee. I suppose she feels protective.'

'If she is fond of Aimee she ought to want to see her happy.'

Cleo chuckled. 'The old one is fond of no one but herself. She thought she was in charge at Belle Rive. Miss Aimee's father spoilt her.'

'I feel very bad about it,' Emma said. 'Perhaps when I leave Esmeralda will go back.'

'She is quite happy where she is. She only misses the power she enjoyed. At one time every man, woman and child in this village was under her thumb. She was queen of them all and they were frightened of her. There are still a few who fear her but the new generation go to school and learn to be Christians. They aren't afraid of the old witch.'

'Did Aimee go to school with the village children?'

Cleo glanced at her swiftly. She hesitated then said carefully, 'No. Her mother thought it best to keep her at home.'

'It didn't harm her. I was surprised that

she knows so much.'

'Yes. Her mother was a very clever woman. She loved her daughter very much. Although I was younger than she was, she used to confide in me and tell me of her fears for Aimee's future.'

As Emma did not want to get involved with the intricate details about the ownership of the estate she changed the subject and asked Cleo about her own life. The woman appeared relieved that Emma had lost interest in Belle Rive and answered her freely.

It was getting on for five o'clock before Emma left. The village had come to life and she heard women laughing and talking as they entered their shacks. Some had returned from work and others had just come off the bus after shopping in Roseau.

Emma smiled at them as she passed. She knew a few because she had often been to the village with Aimee. She quickened her steps thinking that she had stayed too long. Steve and Aimee would be back soon and she had intended to have a meal ready for them. Cassie would not prepare anything for she had not been given any instructions. She might think that they would stay in Roseau until late. Emma frowned. Perhaps they will, she thought. I'm silly hurrying like this. Yet they did go off early. It will be a long day. I expect they are on their way home now.

She crossed the suspension bridge without lingering this time and hurried up the path which would take her out on to a wider lane. It had evidently been part of an estate at one time because either side were the loveliest shrubs all in full bloom. Emma recognized some of them, jacaranda, frangipani and the rose of Sharon. She had become very intrigued when she first noticed them when they were beginning to flower. Most of the landscape she had seen had been bush or forest, coconut, orange and banana groves. Aimee had some hibiscus, allamanda, jessamine and bougainvillaea near the house but some of the vines were only just beginning to flower.

The island will look beautiful when they all bloom, she thought wistfully. I suppose I'm lucky to have seen these.

She had left the lane and was walking over a grassy, uneven path which dipped before a steep incline ahead. She was so deep in thought that she did not notice that she was being followed by a young, coloured man.

At first when he called out she became afraid and hurried on. Glancing back to see how far away he was she recognized him as

163

a man she had seen working outside the house and she stopped to allow him to catch up with her.

He was a striking-looking man, tall and powerful. If Aimee ever wanted anything strenuous done she always asked Reuben. Emma had noticed him because he always wore white trousers, shirt and plimsolls. She had tried to talk to him but had given up because he knew very little English and she could not understand the Dominican patois.

When he reached her he was breathing heavily as if he had run a long way. She gave him a surprised look wondering whether he had a message from Cleo for her.

'What is it, Reuben?' she asked beginning to be afraid because he seemed so agitated.

He shook his black, curly head and waved his hands about. 'Hurt . . . Miss Aimee . . . hurt!' he gasped.

Emma felt herself go cold with fear. 'Do you mean she has had an accident?' she asked then repeated *'accident!'* in case he had not understood.

He nodded. 'Hurt, bad!' he said as if he had recited the words until he knew them. Then he began to gabble away in his own language.

'Is she at Belle Rive?' Emma stared at him in bewilderment for she knew he could not understand her. 'Belle Rive, is she there?' she asked very slowly.

He shook his head and waved a hand at the left side of the lane. 'I . . . take . . . you,' he said.

Emma frowned as she hesitated. There was dense bush on that side of the track. Surely it would be wiser to return to Belle Rive and get the jeep? she thought.

Coming to a decision she said firmly, 'We will go to Belle Rive,' and began to walk rapidly away.

Reuben stared at her in consternation then ran after her and grabbed her arm. 'Belle Rive, no! Over there, bad accident.' Again he pointed to the left.

'It will be quicker by road.'

He shook his head but she could not be certain that he had understood her. And every time she took a step away from him he became more and more agitated.

'Hurt bad! This way quick. I take you.' He was shouting now.

Steve was with Aimee! The thought caused Emma's throat to constrict with fear. Was he so seriously injured that he couldn't help Aimee? The jeep might not be there when she got to Belle Rive. Steve left it on the plantation sometimes. Try as she might she could not remember having seen it when she left the house.

She said urgently, 'Mr Randell was with her. Did Mr Randell send you? Is he hurt?'

A flicker of fear in the dark eyes confirmed her suspicion. Something dreadful had happened to Steve. Reuben understood the word 'hurt'. He had uttered it several times.

She was trembling so much that her voice shook. 'Take me!' she said, too shocked to reason why Reuben had come for her and not gone to Belle Rive.

He ran back looking for a narrow entrance into the bush. Then satisfied that she was behind him he pushed through the thicket and came out on to a rough winding path. Emma followed urging him to hurry. She could think of nothing except finding Steve and Aimee as quickly as possible.

They had been alternately running and walking for fifteen minutes before she began to realize that something was wrong. Where had Reuben come from? How did he know she was in the village? she asked herself dubiously.

'Reuben!' she had to shout for he was so far ahead. 'Wait!'

When he took no notice she stayed where she was determined not to budge until he had explained. Her ruse was successful for within a few minutes he had returned to look for her.

'Hurry, quick,' he said in his deep voice. 'No time, stop.'

'Why didn't you go to Belle Rive? How did you know where to find me?' She had forgotten that he could not understand her and felt annoyed with herself for not speaking more slowly.

'I know. I told to come.'

Evidently he had gleaned her meaning. She wondered whether he understood more than he pretended.

'Who told you to find me?' she asked.

He shook his head. 'Bad accident. You come.'

Emma sighed with exasperation. She glanced behind her and noticed that the path they had come by was already non-existent. The bushes had sprung back and hidden it.

'Take me back!' she spoke curtly giving him a straight look.

He shook his head. 'No good. This way quick.'

He turned and forged ahead of her. There was nothing for it but to go on. It's because he's so determined that I ought to go with him that I feel something isn't right, she told herself doubtfully. It is possible that Steve and Aimee came home on one of the secondary roads. If they have I wouldn't have found them. Perhaps Reuben does know and I'm being imaginative. He works for Aimee. Most of her employees are loyal. Anyway what would be the point of telling me lies? We have to come out somewhere. Reuben seems to know where he is going.

She was becoming tired. Scrambling through bushes, up and down hills had exhausted her. Surely they must be nearly there? she thought anxiously. I'm not going to be much help in this condition.

A glance at her wrist-watch was of no help. She had smashed the glass and one of the hands was missing. That was when I fell down, she thought dazedly too weary to bother about it.

Reuben was quickening his pace and she was forced to hurry to keep up with him. They seemed to be going higher and higher although the air was still humid. There had been no sign of a stream or waterfall, although she had heard water tumbling as if from a great height.

'Reuben, wait! I can't go so fast,' she shouted after she had slipped and fallen again.

She waited expecting him to return as he had done before. But as the minutes passed and there came no sight of him, her fear grew and grew. The silence in the forest was uncanny. She glanced up at the sky for reassurance but only a roof of green met her eyes.

'Reuben!' She called in a loud frantic voice. 'Reuben, come back!'

She dare not go on in case she missed him. Not that there was much hope of proceeding for she could see no path. The undergrowth was so thick that even the light could not penetrate. It can't be night yet! she thought wildly. Her panic mounted as she waited. I will count to a hundred and if he's not back by then I shall try to find the path we came by, she decided, refusing to dwell on the possibility of not being able to see it. Reuben will notice I'm not following him soon.

She kept reasonably calm as she counted but when she had finished her fears returned and she had to accept that the man was not going to return, indeed, had no intention of doing so. He had tricked her by telling her that Aimee had had an accident. But why? What was the point? She didn't even know the man except by sight.

She sat down at the foot of a tree too overwhelmed to do anything but muse over what had happened. I thought it was peculiar that he didn't want to go to Belle Rive, she thought. He must have followed me this afternoon. He runs so swiftly and quietly. I wouldn't have noticed him. Or perhaps he was in the village when I arrived and someone made the most of the opportunity. Yes, that seems much more likely . . . And I can guess whom it was! She smiled grimly. It could only be Esmeralda. She noticed me as I walked by her shack.

She sighed, fumbled for her handkerchief and wiped her face. It stung as she did so and she guessed it was badly scratched for there was blood on the linen. She felt dirty and sticky and her legs were itching from insect bites.

I have to get out of this confined space, she told herself resolutely. I shall be eaten alive if I stay here. I can see chinks of light so it isn't dark yet. Even now she would not admit that she was lost. Hope springs eternal in the human breast and Emma was not lacking in courage.

She chose the largest chink of light and began to break twigs and branches, methodically disregarding thorn-pierced fingers and bruising branches which would swing back to knock her off balance. Fighting her way through she eventually came out into a less confined space but her heart sank when she saw no path. Trees smothered in vines surrounded her and she was clueless of which direction she ought to take.

Walking at random she eventually found several paths but they all led nowhere. Some came to dead ends in thickets, others just petered out in the undergrowth. She was beginning to despair of ever finding one which would lead her out when she heard the cry of the *coucher soleil.*

She was really frightened then. The bird's long, slow call was a warning that the sun was setting and night not far off. She had heard it often enough to recognize it. She raised her head to listen. There were other sounds which frightened her still more; the loud noise of the cicada and a sharp ringing sound. She remembered Aimee speaking of the clanging beetles who made such a noise before nightfall and she shuddered.

I ought not to move from here, she told herself trying to be sensible. It is fairly open and there's plenty of twigs and leaves. If I hurry I can make something to sit on. I daren't lie down. Heaven knows what horrible creatures are crawling about! I bet most of them come out at night. Oh dear! Best not to dwell on that. They will be more frightened of me. I shall prop myself up against a tree. One that is free from ivy.

When darkness obliterated what light

there had been she congratulated herself on her foresight. The mound she had made was not uncomfortable and if she moved her legs at intervals she would frighten off any inquisitive crawlers who might have designs on her ankles. At least it's not raining and I'm not cold. Someone is sure to find me. Other people have been lost in the forest and been found. But her confidence faltered when she thought of the map she had seen in the hotel at Layou. Printed across the centre had been two words, 'unexplored jungle'.

I will find a path tomorrow, she told herself resolutely. Aimee said anyone lost would be found if they kept to a path. The flies have gone, thank goodness! And there aren't any mosquitoes. All I need is patience. I can't be that far from Belle Rive.

Steve and Aimee returned to Belle Rive just before six o'clock. Aimee had spent the day with her aunt and uncle and was looking very subdued. Steve had not stayed at the Guest House long. The Guidas had been pleasant and thanked him for looking after their niece. He had been surprised that they were so easy to talk to. After what Aimee had told him he had expected some animosity. Señora Guida had told him that she wished to talk to her niece alone so he had taken the hint and gone off to amuse himself elsewhere in town, visiting Ellis and later meeting Brenda.

Cassie was leaving as they drew up in front of the house. She was upset because she had not prepared a meal for them and apologized at length.

'It doesn't matter, Cassie,' Aimee said giving her a friendly smile. 'You weren't to know we would be so late.'

Steve frowned thinking it strange that the girl was making such a fuss. 'Emma's here, isn't she?' he asked abruptly.

'She hasn't come back yet. She went to the village to see my mother.'

'That's good,' Aimee exclaimed. 'I wanted my dress altered as soon as possible. I expect you will see her on your way home.'

Neither Steve nor Aimee thought any more about Emma's absence. Aimee began to prepare a meal for them and Steve went to his room to go through his papers. An hour went by before he returned to the living-room to eat the food Aimee had set on the table.

'Emma ought to be back by now,' he said worriedly.

'I expect she stayed to talk to Cassie.'

'It's seven o'clock!'

'Do have something to eat! She will be all right.'

'I don't feel hungry. Put it back in the oven. I'm going to the village.'

Outside he hesitated. If he took the land-rover he might miss Emma who would be walking back. I have to get to the village and find out whether she left, he thought. It will be quicker by road.

Cleo was astonished when Steve walked in unceremoniously. Cassie guessing why he had come became afraid.

'Hasn't Miss Emma come home yet?' she asked.

'Not when I left. She's not here then? What time did she leave?' Steve asked curtly.

Cleo gasped. 'It was ages ago! Five o'clock at a guess.'

'Did she meet anyone or speak to anyone on her way out of the village?'

'I didn't notice,' Cleo said. 'She seemed in a hurry to get back.'

Steve turned to Cassie. 'Did you notice anything unusual on your way home?'

'No. The only person I saw was Reuben. I met him near the suspension bridge and we walked to the village together.'

Steve frowned. 'What was he doing? I mean was he ahead of you? Did he slow down so that you could catch him up?'

Cassie shook her head. 'He was taking a nap on the verge near the lane. I woke him up.'

'I wonder how long he had been there? He might have seen Emma.'

Cassie stood up. 'I know his shack. I will go and ask him.'

When she had gone Cleo asked anxiously, 'Could something have happened to her?'

Steve's face looked grim. 'It's beginning to look like it. It's a long walk back to Belle Rive and there are a few undesirable characters about.'

'Yes. I've told Cassie she's not to go that way after dark.'

Cassie came in and shook her head at Steve. 'Reuben didn't see her. He had been there about thirty minutes.'

'Thanks, Cassie. I will drive back and see if she's returned. If she hasn't I will get up a search party.'

'The men in the village will help,' Cleo said.

Steve drove back at a reckless speed. His fear mounted with every mile and when he strode into the house and heard that Emma had not returned his face whitened and he was unable to hide his agitation.

'I've never seen you like this before,' Aimee said as she poured out a whisky for him. 'I wouldn't get alarmed yet. Emma may have taken the bus into town.'

'That's unlikely and you know it.' Steve tossed back the drink and put the glass down. 'I can't stay. I have a search party to organize. Delay could be fatal.'

'People have been lost before!' Aimee smiled. 'You are making it too important.'

Steve stared at her, his eyes glinting with anger. 'Everyone's important. I thought you were fond of Emma.'

'I am but I think you are making a fuss. She may walk in here any minute.'

'I hope to God she does. But I'm not banking on it.'

Aimee frowned as he walked out. She followed him to the door and watched him climb into the land-rover. Then with a slight shrug of her shoulders she returned to the living-room and switched on the radio.

Meanwhile Cleo had been making herself useful by getting together some of the men and when Steve arrived they were waiting for him with flares and torches. Searching for people who were lost was something they were familiar with.

'You knew I would come back,' Steve said gruffly.

'I thought it likely. It doesn't take two hours or more to walk to the house. I'm very anxious. I like Miss Emma.'

'Thanks Cleo. Have the men got any ideas where to start?'

'I've been speaking to the women who came off the bus about the time Miss Emma left. They said they saw her cross the suspension bridge.'

'That helps. We can start the other side of the river.'

'It will be difficult in the dark. She could have wandered for miles by now.'

Steve said in a strained voice, 'She might not be far. If she was attacked . . .' He broke off, groaned and put his hand to his face.

'Don't think of that,' Cleo said kindly. 'Good luck! I will be waiting. None of us will sleep tonight.'

After consulting the villagers, Steve decided that they search either side of the path all the way to Belle Rive. It took most of the night for they were thorough, determined not to miss an inch. When dawn broke Steve reluctantly called a halt. The men were looking exhausted and he knew they would not be able to go on any longer.

'Come in and have something to eat and drink,' he said. 'After a couple of hours' sleep we can all start again.'

Awakened by the noise Aimee got out of bed and hurriedly dressed. Steve explained the situation to her and she went willingly to the kitchen to prepare food and drink for the men.

Steve followed her into the kitchen. 'You can see to them on your own, Aimee, can't you? I'm going back to the village.'

'It's hardly light!' she exclaimed. 'Do take a break, Steve.'

'Too much time has elapsed,' he said curtly.

'Emma will wander in on her own I expect.'

'I wish I thought so,' he replied grimly. 'She may be hurt.'

Aimee gave him a swift curious glance. 'Would you do the same for me?'

He looked at her in surprise. 'You are used to the forest. Emma isn't.'

'She soon will be,' Aimee muttered as she turned back to the stove.

'I can't understand your attitude, Aimee!' Steve glared at her then turned and left her.

When Steve explained to Cleo what was happening she stared at him in concern and said anxiously, 'She could be anywhere. If only we knew where she entered the forest.'

'I noticed Reuben wasn't with the search party,' Steve said in a tired voice. 'He works at Belle Rive. Doesn't it strike you as strange?'

She nodded. 'Yes, I'm surprised. He's not the type to refuse to help.'

'It's our only lead. Cassie saw him on her way back. Where does he live?'

'I will take you to his shack,' Cleo said.

A sleepy-eyed woman opened the door to them. She stared at them fearfully.

'Has something happened to Reuben?' she asked.

'Isn't he home?' Cleo asked.

'He left after Cassie spoke to him.'

'Reuben has got something to do with it,' Steve said angrily when they left the woman. 'He's so scared he's decided to clear off.'

'It looks like it,' Cleo replied. She glanced at his haggard face and added softly, 'You ought to rest for a bit.'

He smiled grimly. 'I couldn't. I would have nightmares. I shall have to go back. The men will be waiting for me. It's a pity we didn't speak to Reuben. If we don't know where to search it might take us days.'

'I don't think Reuben's wife knew.'

Cassie was coming out of her shack as they reached it and her mother quickly explained where they had been. The girl was dressed ready for work and seemed startled when she heard that Reuben was missing.

'He used to be friendly with a young man who lives near Roseau. Reuben used to take me there before he met Poppy. It's only a wild guess but I think he might go there.'

'It's worth following up. Would you take me there, Cassie?'

She nodded and walked with Steve to the land-rover. He drove off quickly scattering chickens in all directions.

'Will he talk to you, Cassie?' Steve asked when they were approaching the outskirts of Roseau.

'I hope so. I think he's frightened. He may have seen something. I can't believe he would harm Miss Emma.'

It took a few minutes to rouse the Dominican couple. Cassie knew the young man who opened the door and he stared at her in astonishment.

'Sorry to disturb you, Sawyer,' Cassie said apologetically. 'We are looking for Reuben. Is he here?'

'Did Poppy send you? Reuben is only staying a couple of days.'

'No. Mr Randell wants to ask him something. Would you ask him to come down?'

A man pushed Sawyer aside. He had hurriedly pulled on a pair of trousers and was bare from the waist up.

'I told you all I know,' he said speaking in the local patois.

Steve said quickly, 'You ask him Cassie

where he left Emma?'

Reuben looked so frightened when Cassie questioned him that Steve knew his hunch had been right. Cassie did not give up easily and continued to interrogate the young man who reluctantly and slowly divulged the events which had been enacted the previous day.

Cassie turned to Steve. 'He's very frightened and ashamed. Someone offered him money to take Miss Emma into the bush and leave her there.'

'Tell him he has got to come with us,' Steve said grimly. 'If he doesn't help us he will be in big trouble. Did he say who gave him the money?'

Cassie shook her head. 'No, he won't tell me.'

'That can wait. Come on both of you. There's no time to be lost.'

Even with Reuben's help it took the searchers a long time to find Emma. She had been wandering about all day and was miles away from the place where Reuben had left her.

Steve was savagely furious but kept his anger at bay. He knew that he needed to keep alert and calm if he was to be of any help.

By the end of the day Emma was preparing herself for another frightening and desolate night. She was weary and very hungry and had no enthusiasm or strength left to make her mound of leaves and twigs. Her courage was failing for her spirits were low and she was beginning to be afraid that she would never get out of the forest. When she heard the cicada she sat down and tried to calm her thoughts. I must sleep tonight, she told herself resolutely. I have to be strong enough to walk tomorrow.

When she heard a commotion in the bush behind her she became alarmed and got to her feet thinking that some wild creature might be there. Then her heart leapt with hope and her eyes widened with joy when she saw a man thrust his way towards her. She tried to cry out but her throat was so dry she could not utter a sound.

Another man came through the gap and then another. She heard them shout and tears of thankfulness coursed down her cheeks.

Steve brushed by the men with an eagerness which revealed his anxiety. 'Emma! Thank God we've found you! Are you okay, honey?'

She smiled through her tears and began to move towards him but the effort made her head swim and she swayed. He moved swiftly, caught her up into his arms and gazed at her anxiously.

'I'm all right,' she murmured weakly.

Relief sprang to the tired, blue eyes and some of the strain went from his lean, haggard face. Holding Emma carefully he followed the men back to the dirt track which would take them out of the forest.

It was a long trek to the road where he had left the land-rover but he would not relinquish his burden. With her head nestled against his broad chest Emma closed her eyes and fell into a deep sleep.

CHAPTER EIGHT

When Emma opened her eyes the sun was shining into a room she had never seen before. Noise of some kind had awakened her and she gazed about her feeling extremely puzzled.

It was obvious that she was not at Belle Rive. The bed was wonderfully comfortable and the furnishings were very feminine and attractive. She could hear people talking and laughing, vehicles passing and the toll of a church bell.

The door opened and Brenda came in. She smiled at Emma before she put down the tray she was carrying.

'I guessed you would be awake,' she said. 'You've slept ever since Steve brought you to me. Are you hungry?'

'Am I in your room?' Emma asked as she sat up. She noticed then that she was clad in a pretty nightdress. 'I'm in Roseau? That accounts for the unfamiliar sounds. Why did

Steve bring me here?'

'So, you remember what happened! How do you feel?'

'Light-headed and very bruised. I was terrified I wouldn't be found.'

'I guess you were.' Brenda smiled. 'Drink your tea. I've left some clothes there for you if you want to get up. Steve hasn't brought your things over yet. The bathroom is next door. There's plenty of hot water.'

Brenda was wearing green slacks and a pale green blouse. She looked very attractive with her blonde hair loose about her shoulders. When she went to work she wound it into a knot at the back of her head so Emma guessed she was not going that day.

'I'm going to cook you a huge breakfast,' the Canadian girl drawled. 'Steve said I was to feed you up.'

It was such bliss to lie between sweetly smelling sheets with a soft bed beneath her that Emma was disinclined to move. She drank the tea then lay back for a few minutes relishing the comfort and security. It was the delicious smell of bacon cooking that finally got her out of bed. Only then did she realize how dreadfully bruised and stiff she was.

A hot bath and a few exercises will soon

get rid of the stiffness, she told herself firmly before she weakened and climbed back into bed. Brenda's slacks were a little short for her but otherwise fitted like a glove. The Canadian girl had thought of everything, undies, bobby socks, shoes and a white shirt blouse. How kind she is, Emma thought as she dressed after her bath. I'm being a frightful nuisance. I do hope she's not staying away from work because of me.

'I didn't know you had moved from your hotel,' Emma said as she entered a small kitchen and sat down on a cushioned seat close to a breakfast bar with a laminated surface.

'I moved in a week ago. I've been searching for an apartment for ages. Then out of the blue this place became vacant and I snapped it up. It's rather small but pleasant. It will take time to decorate it. Luckily I had some furniture sent out from home and stored it ready for the move.'

'You were lucky to find one unfurnished,' Emma said thinking it strange that Brenda was settling down in an apartment when Steve wanted her to go back to Canada with him. It indicated that she had refused him or perhaps he had decided to stay on. If he did he might be intending to live in the apartment. The thought made her wince with pain and she stared about her with tear-blurred eyes.

'Are you feeling okay, Emma?' Brenda asked looking concerned. 'You have become very pale.'

'I'm fine. I expect it's because I'm hungry.'

'I bet you are. Do start on the grapefruit. You have loads to eat. I had mine earlier. It's ten o'clock in case you haven't noticed. You slept for twelve hours.'

'I don't remember coming here. Did I pinch your bed?'

'No. You are in the guest room. You are going to be here for a few days. Steve didn't want to take you back to Belle Rive.'

Brenda took a plate from the oven and added three fried eggs to the sausages, bacon and fried potatoes. She poured coffee and milk into Emma's cup and filled the toast rack.

'Gracious! I shall never eat all this,' Emma exclaimed. 'It looks delicious. This is the first bacon I've had since I've been here.'

'Eat, don't talk. You needn't finish all of it. I wasn't sure how much you would need.'

Emma was so hungry that she needed no encouraging. She ate slowly savouring every mouthful. Brenda left her to make the beds and when she returned, eyed Emma's empty plate with satisfaction.

'I stopped only when I knew I could eat a tiny morsel more,' Emma said. 'Someone once told me that it's never wise to feel absolutely complete.'

Brenda chuckled. 'I know what you mean. Hunger makes you eat far too much. But your case is a little different. Are you sure you can't manage a slice of toast?'

'No. It was perfect. I can't thank you enough.'

'You are looking better that's my reward. I guess you were real scared when you discovered you were lost.'

'I wasn't at first but after spending the night in the forest I did become frightened.'

'Yes. The jungle is so dense. Luckily there aren't any wild animals only snakes.'

'Snakes!' Emma's brown eyes widened in horror.

Brenda laughed. 'They are harmless. Most of them are fairly small except the boa constrictor. Even their bite isn't poisonous. You don't see many in the south.'

'Thank goodness I didn't know about the snakes!' Emma exclaimed. 'The insects gave me enough trouble. My legs are swollen with bites. By the way thanks for leaving the soothing ointment ready in the bathroom.'

'Steve said I was to look after you.'

Emma glanced at her curiously. 'Why

didn't he take me back to Belle Rive?'

'Roseau was nearer. Steve will explain everything. He will be here soon.'

'He's going to take me back with him, I suppose.'

'I doubt it. Steve was so exhausted last night that I didn't delay him with questions. He had no sleep either. They searched for you from the time you were missing. That was about seven o'clock.'

'Didn't Reuben tell them where I was?'

Brenda looked at her thoughtfully, 'I don't know. Steve was real upset. I've never seen him so shaken. You are a lucky girl, Emma.'

'I know. I could be out there in the rain forest now. It's going to take a long time to forget it.'

'Everything passes with time.' Brenda's green eyes reflected pain and sadness.

Emma gave her a puzzled glance. Surely she ought to be deliriously happy. Didn't she know how much Steve loved her?

Brenda insisted that Emma rest and would not allow her to help with the dishes. Emma sat in the half-furnished lounge flipping idly through glossy magazines until Brenda came in.

'I shall have to leave you for a while,' the girl told her. 'I have some groceries to buy. If Steve comes give him a drink.'

189

'Can't I come with you?' Emma asked feeling suddenly nervous at the thought of meeting Steve.

'No. You ought not to go out today. I won't be long.'

Emma felt very restless. Reading no longer held her interest. I wish I hadn't got to see Steve, she thought. It's bad enough being here with his fiancée. It's very comfortable and Brenda has been extremely kind but I wish I was back at Belle Rive. What is Aimee going to think? I'm supposed to be keeping her company. The Guidas won't be very pleased with me.

Actually meeting Steve was easier than she had imagined it would be for she soon discovered that he was as nervous as she was. Evidently Brenda had left the door on the latch for he walked in without knocking. He hesitated at the open door of the lounge then walked across to Emma and eyed her with concern.

'I didn't expect to find you up,' he said giving her a faint smile. 'I reckon you look much better than you did when I brought you here.'

'Why didn't you take me to Belle Rive?'

'You needed looking after.'

Emma frowned. 'Aimee and Cassie could have done that.'

He said jerkily, 'I have your things in the car. I will bring them up.'

'No, not yet. I suppose that means you think I ought to stay here.'

'Yes.' He hesitated then went on. 'You will be safer here.'

Emma looked puzzled. 'What do you mean, safer? What about my job?'

'That's okay. I've spoken to Señora Guida and she agrees with me that you ought not to go back. She says she will pay you your salary until the end of May.'

'You both think that Esmeralda will try to harm me? Is that why Reuben went off and left me?'

Steve sat down in the chair near her. 'It wasn't Esmeralda. Why did you think it was her?'

'Cleo said something about the villagers being scared of her. And Cassie had told me she makes sacrifices. I knew she didn't like me and blamed me for having to leave Belle Rive. When I found myself alone in the rain forest I thought she had frightened Reuben so much that he had agreed to lose me.'

'What made you go with him? It seems a crazy thing to do.'

Emma laughed awkwardly. 'It was foolish. I know that. But I was under the impression that there had been an accident. I can't understand Reuben's language and he doesn't speak many words of English. But I understood enough to think that you and Aimee were injured. I thought the land-rover had crashed.'

'Why didn't you go back to Belle Rive?'

'I wanted to. I told Reuben I would get the jeep but he got very agitated and kept waving towards the forest. I thought he was trying to tell me that you had come back on a secondary road, one which I wouldn't be able to find. All I could think of was the two of you lying injured without any help at all. Reuben kept saying it would be quicker to go with him. Eventually I decided to go along with him.' She broke off greatly disturbed and unable to look at him.

'Don't distress yourself,' Steve said gruffly. 'It was a difficult situation to be in.'

Taking courage at the kindliness of his voice she went on, 'I can see now how stupid I was. I've caused everyone so much trouble.'

'No one is blaming you. We are all thankful that you came to no harm. I was so afraid for you.'

'I was more frightened than hurt. I wandered about trying to find a path. I found a stream and was able to have a drink and a wash.' She smiled. 'I was so thirsty I didn't even think about pollution. Yesterday morning I came across a wild banana plant which had two rather dried up bananas on it. I was so hungry I could have eaten anything.'

'If Reuben hadn't told us where he left you it might have been days before we found you.' Steve's fingers clenched over his knees. 'I've never been so worried in my life.'

'I'm so sorry,' Emma said contritely.

'It's over now. Brenda will take care of you. It's fortunate that she had moved in to her new apartment.'

'You still haven't told me why I can't return to Belle Rive. If it wasn't Esmeralda, who was it? I can't believe Reuben would harm me intentionally. I hardly know him.'

Steve looked at her gravely. 'It was a surprise for me so I guess you will be shocked. It was Aimee. She bribed Reuben to tell you those lies and lose you.'

Emma gasped. 'Aimee!' Her eyes widened and her face became paler. 'Why would she do that?'

Steve got up and went across to the drinks cabinet. When he came back he had a small glass of whisky in his hand.

'Drink this,' he said. 'You look as though you need it.'

'Thanks.' Emma sipped it slowly.

Steve watched her anxiously then when she put down the glass, began to explain. 'I have had a few suspicions for some months but did not fully understand until I paid the Guidas a visit just before I came here this morning. Aimee is mentally unbalanced. She has always been so. When she was a child she behaved erratically. That is why she never went to school with the other children.'

'I can't believe it!' Emma exclaimed. 'She's so intelligent.'

'Too much so,' Steve looked grim. 'She is cunning and clever. To deceive me for so long took a skill Aimee had acquired by experience. I was well taken in by her. And I can understand why the Armands gave up without a fight. They had become weary of Aimee's dangerous pranks.'

'Did she put those beetles in my bed?' Emma asked in astonishment.

'Yes and destroyed your letters.'

'Oh dear and I blamed Esmeralda!'

'She's a long suffering old woman. Señora Guida told me that Esmeralda was the only one who could prevent Aimee from playing tricks. She was horrified when you told her that the old woman had gone from the house and could not understand what had

194

kept Aimee so quiet. I didn't tell her about the seedlings. I have no proof but it was probably Aimee.'

'Why would she do that?'

'She doesn't have to have a reason. She gets delight that way.'

'Why didn't her aunt tell me before I came?' Emma said.

'You wouldn't have come, would you? Señora Guida was very worried. She had thought her niece would be safe with the Armands. They knew about Aimee's lapses and could keep her under control. Also with Esmeralda there Señora Guida knew the girl would come to no harm.' Steve smiled wryly. 'I really upset the applecart. No wonder the Guidas were agitated about me. Aimee took me in all along the line.'

Emma said slowly, 'She was very fond of you. If I hadn't turned up she would have deceived you for much longer.'

Steve frowned. 'She didn't do it intentionally. I don't think she realizes she is not as sane as other people. All her friends and relations have taken pains not to treat her too differently. It was the Guidas who deceived us.'

'I suppose it was Aimee who made the other two women leave.'

'I imagine so. I didn't like them much so I

195

didn't take much notice. Now I know the facts I feel real sorry for them. Señora Guida told me that she had informed the other two of Aimee's lapses. She had made light of it saying that they happened infrequently and she soon recovered. That's why they both behaved so peculiarly. And because they left so quickly the Señora decided not to tell you. She thought that because you were sensible and not excitable you would be good for her niece. I'm afraid I became angry when she told me that. She took unfair advantage of you and I told her so.'

'It was difficult for her. Her husband was ill and she couldn't leave him to look after Aimee.' Emma was silent for a few moments then exclaimed, 'That's why Aimee wasn't left the estate!'

'Yes. Her parents came to an agreement with the Guidas when Aimee was fourteen. They were worried because they knew she would not be able to run the estate. If anything happened to them Señora Guida was to have the estate on the understanding that she would care for Aimee and make provision for her future. At the time I don't suppose any of them thought it would happen so soon.'

'Aimee's father didn't leave anything to

chance, did he? He gave her the house in case the relations didn't keep to their bargain.'

'That was her mother's doing. It's real sad. They were such a charming family.'

Emma remarked idly, 'Brenda's a long time. I thought she would be back by now.'

'I told her not to come back for a couple of hours. I met her in the town. She's an understanding person.'

'Were you upset when she moved from her hotel and came here?' Emma asked curiously.

'Why would I be upset? It's much more convenient for her.'

Emma looked down at her hands unable to meet his puzzled eyes. 'I thought you wanted her to go back to Canada with you.'

'No, not Brenda! For Pete's sake! Is that what you have been thinking? Is that why you've been so difficult?'

She raised her head and stared at him in astonishment then after a slight pause said, 'Aimee told me soon after I came that you and Brenda were in love.'

'Aimee!' He smiled twistedly. 'I might have known! And all the time she was sympathizing with me.'

'Why?' Emma asked in bewilderment.

Steve's blue eyes glinted. 'You're not

unintelligent. You must have figured there was something between us. You and I . . . honey! Aimee knew I loved you. She kept telling me how crazy that guy Forbes was about you and that you were real upset because he was not staying long.'

'Oh dear!' Emma ejaculated. 'Aimee is clever. She's been fooling both of us.'

He studied her confused face watching the delicate rose colour rise to her cheekbones and released an imprisoned breath. Then as if he could stand the silence no longer he got to his feet and pulled her up beside him.

'Am I reading the signs correctly, honey?' he asked hoarsely. 'You do care for me, after all?'

She did not have to reply. His answer was in her adoring brown eyes. Then she was in his arms receiving passionate, hungry kisses which set her body aflame.

She drew back breathless and trembling, gazing up at his lean, bronzed face in wonder. 'It's incredible!' she murmured.

Steve's eyes twinkled. 'See what you've missed by being so obstinate.' He smiled tenderly and rested his face on her hair. 'You were so evasive. I could never get you alone.'

'It was difficult. You went to see Brenda

so often. What could I think? She's so attractive.'

Steve grinned. 'I've never liked blondes. Brenda and I are good friends.' He sat down and pulled Emma into the space beside him. Then with his arm across her shoulders went on, 'She's a real unhappy lady. Life hasn't been too good to her. Her husband went off with another girl a couple of years after their marriage.'

'I didn't realize how unhappy she was until today. I wish I had known,' Emma said regretfully.

He chuckled. 'If you had, things might have been different. I wouldn't have had to endure so much frustration. Sometimes it was difficult to be polite to anyone.'

Emma laughed. 'I noticed. You were terribly grumpy some days.'

'Can you wonder at it? All I got from you was suspicious or cold glances. You didn't really fall for that guy Forbes, did you?'

'No. He was kind and I liked him but I was in love with you. I really wanted to go with you to Trafalgar Falls. Then when I thought of Brenda I knew it would have been foolish.'

'She was the reason I came back to the island. Ellis has been a buddy of mine for years. He was offered a post over here and when Brenda decided to pack up and come with him he asked me to tag along. We've both done our best to give her a good time. It's a humbling experience for anyone to know that the person you love prefers someone else. We tried to fill in the gap in her life, fairly successfully, I guess. She is now taking a fresh interest in life and has a small circle of friends. I'm not needed now.'

'So that was your main reason for becoming Aimee's manager!'

'No. I didn't intend to stay so long. Aimee's parents had been so good when I came here before. I felt I owed them something.'

'You have more than paid your debt. Did Aimee know about Brenda's husband?'

'She did. I explained that I intended taking her about until she became used to being on her own.' He bent his head and kissed her. 'Aimee told you differently, I reckon.'

Emma said seriously, 'You could have told me yourself.'

'It didn't seem important. How was I to know you were worrying about it. You gave me the cold shoulder when I tried to be friendly. I didn't think I had much chance with you.'

'Were you going to let me go back without

telling me?'

'No. Stop teasing! If you had gone without telling me I would have come after you. Coming back with Aimee the day you disappeared I made up my mind to have it out with you. I couldn't stand the uncertainty any longer.'

'What did Aimee say when her aunt told her she was going to sell the estate?'

'She became very quiet. I think it changed her. She acted real strange after we got back.'

'It could have been because of me.'

'It was more than that. I can't explain exactly. I felt I didn't know her.'

'I experienced the same feeling once or twice. Didn't you ever notice the way the villagers spoke of her? They spoke of her as if they were talking about a child.'

'I've never thought that. The villagers are real loyal. Not one of them told me of Aimee's history.'

'What will happen to her now?'

'She is going to stay at Belle Rive. Her aunt has decided not to sell the estate. I think Aimee's latest escapade has frightened her. She didn't realize the girl might harm anyone.'

Emma said thoughtfully, 'I can see now why she did it. She was jealous of me. She didn't want you to leave and she thought I was the reason you were going.'

'I would have gone anyway.'

'Aimee wouldn't believe that. She was very possessive regarding you. I don't think you realize how much she thought of you.'

'I was beginning to see things more clearly and I wasn't looking forward to the time when I would have to go.'

'Are you going to continue to manage the estate?'

Steve nodded. 'It's only for another week. Armand and his wife are going to take over then. Señora Guida and her husband are moving in to Belle Rive today.'

'Esmeralda seems to be the one who has suffered the most,' Emma said reflectively.

'She's going back too. Señora seemed certain that the old woman would want to go.'

'She might take some persuading. She's annoyed with Aimee.'

'When you care for someone you don't hold on to resentment. It will be a darn sight more comfortable at Belle Rive.'

'What has happened to Reuben?'

'He's back with his wife. You don't want to punish him do you?'

'No. I want to forget all about it.'

'That's what I thought. He's been badly

frightened and he has to live down his fall from grace. The villagers won't let him off easily.'

'Why were you so worried the day we went to the cinema? Did you suspect Aimee then?'

'Only vaguely. Cassie had seemed anxious when you were away so long and I asked her why. She was reluctant to tell me but eventually said that she was frightened Miss Aimee might do something foolish. I was surprised and asked her to explain, but she wouldn't tell me any more. Señora Guida told me this morning that Aimee was liable to act wildly at times and when she was a child she often frightened the village children.'

'It's very sad and confusing. I suppose we have been lucky that she behaved normally most of the time.'

'We weren't expecting her not to act sanely, so I guess we didn't notice small incidents. She was cunning enough to hide her real intentions.'

Emma said regretfully, 'I feel so sorry for her. I suppose it wouldn't be wise to see her?'

Steve bent his head to touch her cheek with his lips. 'No, it wouldn't, honey. By now she's forgotten what she did to you. It wouldn't be fair to remind her and for the same reason I reckon we ought to wait to get married.'

Emma stared at him with mingled surprise and excitement. 'You wanted us to marry here?'

'Sure, why not?'

She laughed. 'It's rather quick, isn't it? I haven't many clothes here and I haven't got used to the idea yet. I'm still feeling dazed.'

'I don't want to be separated from you. We could have got married and had a few days honeymoon here.'

'It's a small place. Aimee would have heard about it and been very hurt. I couldn't do that to her.'

'I guess not. Next thing you will be telling me you want to go back home first.'

'I ought to. I left my clothes with my parents. They will be wanting to see me. It would be better if I went home first. You could go back to your ranch and I could come out to you later.'

'That's out for a start!' Steve said firmly. 'If you are determined to go back to England, I shall tag along with you. There are too many eligible males in London.'

Emma chuckled. 'I never found them.'

'Forbes lives there doesn't he?'

'You are still jealous of him! He didn't

mean anything to me.' She looked at him seriously and spoke in a low, soft voice, 'I'm old-fashioned, Steve. I shall always love you, whatever happens. If we do have differences, as I expect we shall, it won't be because I've become interested in another man.'

He remained silent so moved by her declaration that he felt humble and inadequate. His arm tightened about her and he rested his head on her red-gold hair.

'Do whatever you want to, honey,' he said quietly.

She smiled. 'I would prefer you to come home with me. But if you have to get back to your ranch then I will come with you.'

He grinned, pulled her on to his knees and kissed her hard. 'My sister and her husband won't mind waiting a few more days. At the end of the week I will take you back to see your parents. I guess you'd like to marry there. When that's accomplished we can fly back to Manitoba and begin a new life together.'

'You mentioned you had two sisters. Are they both at the ranch?'

'No. Jean left home at the same time I did. She's teaching in Montreal. I was always closer to Molly. She married one of my buddies, Ritchie. You will like them. They aim to settle somewhere near home. They have had a struggle to get what they want. They married too young and Ritchie's parents haven't been able to help. I'm not too badly off that's why I offered to buy a ranch for them. They will pay me back in time.'

'It is generous of you,' Emma remarked. 'Molly is lucky. Not many brothers would do as much.'

'They have helped me. I couldn't have gone off as I did. When Pa died I wasn't ready to settle down to ranching. Molly and Ritchie had a couple of kids and no prospects. I took the opportunity that was there. You could say it was a selfish offer. When I was a lad I wanted to be a logger.' Steve grinned. 'I soon discovered my mistake. It was a tough life. Then I took up forestry and began to travel. It was good while it lasted. I didn't intend to use up too many years. If it hadn't been for Brenda and Aimee I would be in Manitoba now.'

Emma sighed. 'We wouldn't have met. We wouldn't have known either of us existed.'

'It's been a frustrating year but worthwhile. I knew that the minute I clapped eyes on your red head.'

Emma laughed. 'No one would have guessed it! You were downright rude. You made me feel two inches high.'

'I was annoyed because I had to meet you.

After the other two young women, I reckoned I had had enough.' He smiled. 'It didn't take me long to discover how different you were. After a couple of weeks I fumed at the delay. I'm an impatient guy, you see.'

'I know! I'm surprised you didn't declare yourself and whisk me away protests and all.'

'I guess that's what I would have liked to have done. I was too scared. It was the most important thing that had ever happened to me. I couldn't risk refusal.'

'It doesn't matter now. I hope Brenda won't mind me staying for a few days with her.'

'She's only too pleased to help. When she comes back I will take you both out to lunch.'

'I shall have to change first.'

'You look fine to me. Do you have to?'

Emma struggled up on to her feet. She glanced down at the slacks Brenda had lent her and chuckled.

Steve grinned. 'I see what you mean. Okay, I will go and get your baggage.'

He strode to the door, hesitated then went back and kissed her. 'I guess the novelty will wear off,' he drawled. 'Even a few minutes away from you is unbearable.'

She smiled tenderly as she watched him go from the room. Steve was everything she could wish for in a man, strong, kind, generous, understanding . . . there was no end to his qualities. And he loved her!

She stood quite still delighting in the thought, marvelling that it could be so. The events leading up to this morning had opened up a dazzling future new and exciting. She was no longer alone. Now she had Steve to guide and counsel her and love her. And she would do anything for him for she loved him so much that it hurt.

Steve came in and dropped her cases on the floor. He gave her a twinkling glance.

'Did you miss me?' he asked.

Emma nodded. 'It was too long,' she replied softly.

He smiled tenderly and enfolded her in his arms. Emma raised her head, her eyes alight with happiness. It was all she wanted, a lifetime spent with the man she loved.

We hope you have enjoyed this Large Print book. Other Thorndike, Wheeler, and Chivers Press Large Print books are available at your library or directly from the publishers.

For information about current and upcoming titles, please call or write, without obligation, to:

Publisher
Thorndike Press
295 Kennedy Memorial Drive
Waterville, ME 04901
Tel. (800) 223-1244

or visit our Web site at:

www.gale.com/thorndike
www.gale.com/wheeler

OR

Chivers Large Print
published by BBC Audiobooks Ltd
St James House, The Square
Lower Bristol Road
Bath BA2 3SB
England
Tel. +44(0) 800 136919
email: bbcaudiobooks@bbc.co.uk
www.bbcaudiobooks.co.uk

All our Large Print titles are designed for easy reading, and all our books are made to last.